Nightmare Seasons

Charles L. Grant

TOR

A TOM DOHERTY ASSOCIATES BOOK

NIGHTMARE SEASONS

Published by arrangement with Doubleday & Company, Inc.

A Tor Book

Published by Tom Doherty Associates, 8-10 W. 36th St., New York, N.Y. 10018

First printing, May 1983

ISBN: 0-523-48076-8

Printed in the United States of America

Distributed by Pinnacle Books, 1430 Broadway, New York, N.Y. 10018

*For Bob and Mary, who by reason of insanity have
put up with me more than any couple
should, especially when I killed Bob
off in Wyoming*

PROLOGUE

Winter . . . and rain.

During the blade-sharp days of a January cold snap, during the hours when snow immobilizes and breath turns to short-lived fog, there are the dreams of summer, of green, of walking with no particular purpose except to savor across the playing fields of the park beneath hickory and ash and white birch of such luxuriantly thick foliage that even the still air seems hazed with mint. In part it is a steeled defiance of a numbing temperature that reduces animals to hibernation and man to bitter complaint; and in part it is a hypnotic gesture to the pleading of one's senses for an earnest reassurance that this sort of weather will not last, that there will indeed be a time when warmth beyond the hearth is a reality in spite of the fact that it seems now like nothing more, and nothing less, than an attic memory.

But there are worse times than the cold.

And there are worse illusions than memory.

There are the cruel teasing thaws that defy the season with a mercury grin; thaws that banish the snow, fill the streams, oft-times clear the sky to a taunting deception of June's soft blue.

And when there is no blue, there is the rain.

A lifeless, persistent, two weeks' rain that begins without warning as a twilight mist and becomes during slumber an early-dawn drizzle lightly coating even the most pristine white with a dull ghostshroud of grey. It begins lightly, silently, and suddenly grows mad. Winds shift and rise, clouds darken and spill, and gutters hold too much, storm drains not enough, while the ground at every corner becomes brown and soggy and bespeaks the Brontës' moors.

There is, then, a lethargy, an apathy, when even the best of relationships is strained to the breaking because there is *warm* out there beyond the streaking condensation on the windows, a *warm* that in its taunting is a lie, and a rain that gives no life.

For some . . . for many, the obvious escape is in sleep beneath down quilts and electric blankets and in huddling and in dozing (though the dreams that they wish for are not always the dreams they receive); for others there is the mechanical and time-killing routine of nine to five, a liturgy of complaints, a ritual of wishes; and for still others who have the luck and the means there is the literal escape to climes that still know the sun (though the escape they perform is as brief as the false thaw).

And finally, for those like me who take the seasons as they come, there are voyages in books. When the house grows too small and the shadows too real and the clock in the hallway talks death to itself. When the oven is merely hot and the sheets merely stiff and the clock in the hallways talks death to itself. When the floorboards creak and the furnace pops and the eaves sigh and the windows are too blind . . . and the clock in the hallway talks death to itself.

Winter . . . and rain.

It is a time, then, for research, and for prodding myself into getting away from staring at the backs of my hands and cracks in the walls and back into the business that lets me live; and after two full days of burying myself rather effectively and productively in the Oxrun Station library, Nat Clayton took pity on my aching spine and piles of notes scattered over the blondewood table and brought me a sandwich from the corner luncheonette. She was the first person I had met when I'd moved to the Station, and I was the only one she had told about the losing of the index finger on her left hand. Her soft sable hair was cut long for the winter, and there were more times than one when I envied husband Marc for the partner he had. Marc, on the other hand, envied my employment.

Neither of them, however, envied the stories I told.

The sandwich.

I grinned at Nat, probably stupidly, and ate while I leafed through an unnecessarily dry volume of Connecticut history. It was one of those moments when I was not exactly sure what I was looking for, one of those moments when I would know when I found it. A vague idea for the next book was swimming uncharitably distantly, and with luck I was hoping my browsing would find its definition. If it happened today, I had promised myself, I would begin work on that instead of the more commercial, bills-paying one I had under contract.

Not that I ever did less than the best a book called for.

But once in a while I wanted to have fun.

Especially now, in the rain and the warm/cold that

made even the likes of Oxrun Station a place to ride by on the way to someplace bright.

An hour later, sandwich devoured and the history book closed in admission of failure (not to mention procrastination), I had resigned myself to a bout of artistic self-pity, with a few rounds of hearty depression thrown in for the crowd. And again it was dear Nat who saw my distress and realized it was a time when I could be interrupted without harm.

She came away from the horseshoe-shaped main desk and stood in front of me, holding out a book in her left hand. It was a slim volume, expensively bound in deep ebony leather, and the pages were virtually onionskin and edged with gold. The look of it demanded cautious handling, which I gave it while she told me how she had come by it.

"See, I was supposed to be getting something on Frost," she said with a grin that anticipated one of my patented, cheap wisecracks. When it didn't come, however, she only shrugged and touched thoughtfully at her cheek. "I tell you, I really do like Iris and Paul, no kidding. I mean, that store's the best thing that ever happened to them since Paul retired. And don't get me wrong, I think they've done a hell of a job there since Cyd . . . well, since she took off like that for God knows where. But sometimes . . . I mean, really. I ask for Robert Frost, for crying out loud, and I get something like this." She gestured at the book as though it were a dead mouse. "Don't know why I let Paul talk me into keeping it." She gestured again, this time nervously. "Anyway, I started to read it last night, thought about you right away, and when I told Marc, he said I should let you have a look."

I closed the book carefully.

"Oh, go ahead," she said when I tried to push it back into her hand. "Go on, take it home. Really. It isn't going to bite you, you know."

I backed off slightly, palms up and out and shaking my head. "Nat, you are talking to the world's most accomplished fumbler and rare things destroyer. Olympics-class, at least. I have won gold medals for dropping a four-hundred-page unbound manuscript in the middle of Madison Avenue. I have been cited by world leaders for dropping Dresden china and signed crystal. I cannot comb my hair without first cracking my knuckles on the brush. No. I don't want any part of this, m'dear."

"Take it," she said. And at least she had the grace not to laugh at my wriggling unease.

"No, damnit. That thing there is much too expensive: all you have to do is look at it to know that. Nope. I don't want it. I don't even want to breathe on it. But as long as it's yours," I added quickly, "what you should do, you know, is display it here, in a glass-fronted bookcase or something like that."

She shook her head. The damned woman was actually enjoying herself.

"Natalie, please . . ." And I spread my hands over my notebooks, trying for the perfect attitude of supplication. "Look at all this stuff, huh? Do you have any idea what work I have to do now just to set things up? I've got to sort it, file it, absorb it, recheck it, rearrange it and then start writing. I wish I could help you, but I haven't got the time, believe me. Thanks for the thought, but really, no."

I looked away and began shuffling papers and note

pads into something that looked like an official pile. I kept shaking my head—slowly, so she would think I was bemoaning the work yet to come when I got home.

Unfortunately, she knew me too well. She took the chair opposite and placed the book between us. She said nothing. She only stared.

Against all regulations I lit a cigarette, watched the smoke cloud her face, watched the book catch the light. I sniffed. I cleared my throat. I patted my shirt pocket to be sure my pen was there. "What's it about?"

"Seasons."

I squinted. "Seasons? What do you mean, seasons? Good lord, Nat, it isn't poetry, is it?"

She shook her head. My left hand disobeyed orders and reached out, pausing only when I saw her grin.

"Take it," she insisted gently. Then she glanced toward the tall, arched windows that made up the building's front wall. "It's the weather for it, believe me."

I knew then there was no sense at all in trying to protest any further. Natalie was, among many other delightful and possibly sinful things, one of the most stubborn people I have ever met. If she was convinced that I would enjoy this book, then that was the end of it.

It did not occur to me until much later that "enjoy" was a word she had not used once.

I fussed around for another half an hour, just to show her the sacrifice I would be making through the loss of much-needed time to work, and walked back home. I ate. Showered. Defied the latest statistics and sat in front of the television set with the screen blank. And once I felt comfortable enough I picked up her book.

From Poe to Dunsany, Lovecraft to Bloch, there have

been manuscripts and tomes found in bottles, chests, closets, desks, canes, candles, woodwork, hearths, musty shops tucked away on side streets no one ever noticed, and ships' holds filled with scrabbling rats and stagnant water. All of them, according to the discoverer, emit a rather unwholesome and indefinable aura, enticing the reader deep into the supposed terrors therein, preternaturally seizing the imagination and wringing it dry of every vestige of emotion, of reason, of nightmares long dormant. And more often than not the manuscript turns lethal.

This volume, however, was nothing more than raised cool leather in my hands. Light, unimposing, handled cautiously only because I was afraid to do it damage and be damned for my clumsiness. I turned it around several times—front to back, side to side—and held it close to my eyes while I leaned back toward the lamp. I touched gingerly at the gold edges. I rubbed a finger against my chest, then brushed it timidly over the tooling. I turned it again. Twice more. Once brought it to my nose to sniff for age. Then placed it in my lap and stared at it.

There was no title.

There was no mention of an author.

I rubbed my thumb over my chin, scratched at an eyebrow, took my glasses off and cleaned them. Then with a sigh loud enough to alert the world to the birth of a new martyr, I picked it up again.

Nothing on the first five pages but yellowing age stains and blotches of what might have been perspiration, or tears; nothing quite so dramatic as dried smears of blood.

A private edition, apparently, albeit one of reasonably respectable age and involved wealth.

The printing was so finely done it seemed etched on water, but there were no illustrations or illumination work.

I read quickly at first, not really slowing down until I realized with a somewhat delighted start that this was a series of accounts of Oxrun Station and how it had been at various moments in its recent past.

I do not say "history"; there are too many implications of truth in that word.

Yet, to be honest, it did not give me, simply by holding it, uneasy sensations of shadows pressing over my shoulder, or unnameable presences lurking about my windows. It was, I judged, a book and nothing more. And like all books, it could do nothing to me that I did not permit.

And so, with cigarettes and a not-so-fine brandy to hand, I read it.

Forgetting the time, and the cigarettes, and the brandy, and the cold.

But not forgetting at all that I was still in Oxrun Station.

And it was winter . . . and it was raining.

PART I

Spring, 1940

THOU NEED NOT
FEAR MY KISSES,
LOVE

Moving

The wind in slowtime to the drift of the night's clouds. It barely shifted the clinging spring mist that hung over the Station, barely chilled the uncomfortably early heat the afternoon's long rain had been unable to banish.

The wind in slowtime. Touching the back of an ear like a feather, trying to budge the nightweight of a curl.

The wind . . . in slowtime.

Yet there were gusts on occasion, and a few that were quite strong, though they seemed less demonstrations of strength than measures of desperation. Gusts that chased a huddled white cat from beneath a dripping hedgerow, tested panes and twigs and found shallow voice in the throat of a black alley. A battered paper cup rimmed brown with dried coffee was tripped off a curb on Centre Street and nudged fitfully along the lane of a gutter through damp islands of mud and debris unidentified and shimmering in the frayed glare of a streetlamp; nudged and herded to the bars of a corner storm drain where it caught, balanced, blew briefly into the street before being recaptured and returned with a vengeance; returned and held, tipped . . . and gone.

Sam watched the greywhite container flash brightly
before vanishing. Then she wrenched away suddenly
and hunched her shoulders against the wind. Waited.
Muttered. Heard from a nearby home whose radio was
too loud the falsely idyllic strains of a slowtime "South
of the Border." A window abruptly slammed shut; the
music sliced to silence. It would be just her luck, she
thought sourly, that a war would start tonight and she
would not know it.

She waited.

The wind gusted.

And when the air at last calmed with its mocking reminder of a winter just past, she straightened and
frowned, craning her neck as though a cramp had
begun. Her left hand touched absently at the pale pink
kerchief protecting her short hair, then dropped to
adjust the collar on her new spring coat more snugly
around her throat. It was fur, and it was damp, and it
was beginning to smell.

The frown deepened to a scowl. The soft planes of her
face were given harsh edges, and her age increased as
her irritation grew.

Above her head, in a grey marble casing with false
turrets atop, the bank clock chimed softly, barely
warning the night. It was nine. He was late.

She tugged at an earlobe to mark her annoyance,
swept an auburn curl away from her right eye. She
paced to the corner and made a savage survey of the
street before wandering back to the bank and leaning
hard against its wall. He was late. If she hadn't had so
much to do at the office, she could have arranged to
meet him at home, in comfort. Nevertheless, he was
late. But not to worry. Not yet. Not . . . yet.

An automobile passed. A coupe. A Pontiac. Tensing slightly, she squinted to find its color, found it wrong and shrugged. Five minutes later a touring car swept by. She ignored it; it was traveling too fast. Her cheeks puffed and she blew a hard breath, and it occurred to her then that a patrol car might pass. She grinned at the thought. Maidens lounging on street corners were not functions of the Station.

And the way things were going she would probably know the patrolman:

—Hey there, Miss England, you waiting for a bus?

—Very funny, Thomas. I'm waiting for Malcolm Marsh, in fact.

—Out here in the rain?

—It isn't raining, it's drizzling. Don't you ever listen to the weather reports?

—Well, look, Miss England, don't you think . . . I mean, don't you think it might be a better idea if you waited over there in the luncheonette? It's drier, trust me, and you can see this spot just as well.

—Thomas Hancock, Officer, sir, are you worried about my virtue?

A car's horn sounded harshly somewhere deeper in the village; it was answered by another, and ringed by faint laughter. She shook her head vigorously to dispel her fancies and glanced up at the clock again. Fifteen past. Not to worry. Especially tonight. Tonight, she had promised herself before leaving the office, she would not be waiting around long enough for worry to take hold. As she had let her coworkers know in no uncertain terms, this was to be his last chance, and it appeared that her suspicions were proving unpleasantly, and disappointingly, correct—that Malcolm Marsh knew far less about her affections and their direction than his ego led him to believe. That she was unmarried, and in her mid-thirties, had evidently gained her unwanted admittance to a club of stereotypes, and unafraid to unleash her intelligence in the presence of others, made her somewhat of a curiosity, and suspect. At least as far as Malcolm was concerned.

A challenge, then, and Samantha was just perverse enough to give it to him.

As she granted him ten minutes more, to nine twenty-five.

He took it without asking, and five minutes besides.

A snub-nosed bus lumbered by, the last connection the Station had with the outside, and she was reminded for no reason at all of the Saturday a number of her friends had chartered one such for a trip down to the Bronx Zoo. It had started as a lark—why should kids have all the fun?—and became a serious tour. They'd felt foolish piling out at the entrance, watching all the gawkers waiting for the children, less so once they'd begun their walking. Vince Bartelle had stayed with her most of the day, commenting often, making Malcolm angry at the outrageous lies he told when the facts eluded him. The only time Vince had quieted stretched across the homes of the big cats and the snakes. He remarked on the difference between the cats eating their food dead while the snakes ate it alive, was fascinated when Malcolm explained that many species of serpent had quite a number of teeth, much more than the two fangs they were usually associated with. At the monkey house Vince sported and Malcolm grunted. She loved the elephants, and Vince regaled her with the exploits of Sabu until Malcolm coldly muttered that Hollywood didn't know a tusk from a tuba. Vince told him he had no soul, and for the first time Sam wondered just how much Malcolm loved her.

Five minutes.

Great, she thought; this is just great. The biggest movie in the whole damned world finally gets around here and I have to miss it. It wasn't Gable so much that she minded not seeing, nor the elegant and tragic Leslie Howard, nor the famed, delicious moment of swearing; it was the color. In this new season when all colors were still struggling to be green and there were still too many shades of brown left over from the cold, she wanted the color. So she told herself when she gave him still another five minutes for penance, and one for absolution.

—Hey, Miss England, you going into business for yourself out here?

—Not funny, Tom.

—Sorry, Miss England.

—So am I, Tom. But at least I have company.

She decided then that one of these days she was going to have to let Hancock take her out, just so she wouldn't have conversations with him on drenched street corners on a Friday night—especially when he wasn't even there to talk to.

What, she wondered suddenly, is the legal age when one officially becomes a spinster?

She scowled at herself in a warning against self-pity and considered lighting a cigarette. No; *L.S.M.F.T.*, perhaps, but Lucky Strikes were decidedly not the fashion for ladies at night in Oxrun Station. And definitely not out in the open.

A moment later she grinned and shook her head

slowly, a gesture of concession: the problem was not Malcolm Marsh, nor her insanity in waiting in the rain like some lovesick schoolgirl. The problem, as it had been for the last two or three weeks, was the house—a porched Cape Cod, comfortably furnished, flanked by dogwood and red maple and ringed by a privet hedge that gave fits to the neighbors' dogs. A thoroughly pleasant place to live, and she did not want to go home.

Damnit, Malcolm, I was counting on you!

The window down the street opened again and she heard someone's halting rendition of the new Goodman tune. She hated it. The window closed. She wondered if it was a sign.

She took a deep breath, held it, hoped she would not meet anyone from the office. The people she worked with had not been taken with Malcolm from the first day he'd come in to keep a luncheon date, and even Danny, the odd-jobber, had managed to hint to her that she was wasting her time. It galled her to think that a kid might be right.

She glanced up at the clock; enough was enough.

With hands buried deeply in her coat pockets, head down to avoid the wind and watch for puddles, she walked quickly down Centre Street to Chancellor Avenue and turned right, in front of the police station. She tried not to think of having just stood the man up—or of having been stood up in turn—or of the house and her unreasonable reluctance to face it. Instead, she concentrated on her summer vacation. A year ago she had promised herself a first-class sleeper to Los Angeles, or perhaps a visit to some old Holyoke friends who had settled in the Pacific Northwest. But at the time there had been, suddenly, too many variables in too many portfolios for her to leave the brokerage house for an extended absence. This year, however, things were going to be different.

Maybe, she thought, he's been in an accident.

The house . . .

There had also been the matter of Vincent Bartelle. He had joined the firm last May at the insistence of her uncle, who was still nominally in charge, though he was and would be until he died confined to his bed and left the daily operations to herself and Reginald Craig. As soon as Vince had seen her he had wanted her, and made no bones about it. Yet there was an Old World courtliness about him that kept her from feeling constantly on the defensive, constantly threatened. So, there had been a dinner. Two. An average of once a month throughout the winter after the excursion to the zoo. Then, last month, he had asked her if she would like an ocean voyage to Southampton. England, that is, he'd said with a poke at her nameplate on her office door. You and me, kiddo, what do you say? She had been so unnerved she'd almost said yes.

Maybe, she thought, he got his signals crossed and he's waiting at the house.

She crossed the street without looking, and slowed as she reached the newly built hospital. Her gaze touched at each window light and dark, reflex prodding a smile for each couple she passed.

Her third choice was to stay home. To catch up on her reading. To finish that ridiculous rug still half hooked and draped forlornly over the back of a kitchen chair. The garden would want tending. The porch cried for painting, the attic for cleaning . . . Vince, however, would not wait for her answer. Yesterday, he had dropped a grinning hint that he was asking an acquaintance who lived across the state in Hartford. She did not mind, not all that much. Despite the crunch, her savings were more than adequate for the train journey westward. But her nerves were not. She had been too long in the Station, she told herself, far too long in relative isolation, and she was not all sure she could handle the world yet. Small doses first. Harley. Hartford. Boston. New York. By the time she was able to survive a week alone in Manhattan . . .

A laugh as small as her smile escaped her. In part it was at her own marvelous performance in rationalization, in part the sight of Malcolm's bulbous automobile parked at the curb in front of the house, the last on the block just before the deep woods. So he *had* been confused. How like the man, she thought with a surge of affection that both startled and disturbed her.

She stopped at the passenger door and leaned down. There was no one inside.

On the porch, then. Like an old man he would be in that bentwood rocker he had staked out for his own, his freckled brow familiarly creased in perpetual scowling, right hand imperially on the armrest, left pulling absently at the knot of his tie. Even in a furnace Malcolm would always wear a tie.

She straightened, turned, and would have called out. She shivered instead.

It was the silence that stilled her.

No automobiles passing the corner, no nightbirds or insects, not a single vagrant droplet falling from a leaf.

The last house on the block.

To her right was the village, to the left the woodland that tangled up to the hills surrounding Oxrun on three of its sides. The house opposite had burned down five years before; the very day, she recalled, that the WPA was formed and her uncle had his stroke. The only other house whose residents she knew was directly next door, the Kramers' small Colonial—and they were down in Virginia visiting their children.

Her hands left their pockets and crossed over her stomach.

The quiet.

Even during the day the birds seemed to avoid her, birds that had once filled the trees to distraction and had made her believe a cat might be a fine and ruthless investment.

When she took a step away from the car, her heel cracked too loudly and she stopped again, waiting.

The quiet.

Her own place. The porch partially screened by evergreen shrubs whose names she despaired of ever remembering, whose branches she was barely able to keep in close check. The amber light over the front door was burned out again. The windows were blind. The hedge that marked her front lawn could easily have been stone.

She thought about walking down to the Kramers' and whistling for their old tom, a one-eyed bloated animal she had promised to keep fed while its owners were away. But the cat had never liked her, and now that she thought about it she hadn't seen it since last Monday.

Another deep breath, then, and a silent scolding for her fears. A step toward the front walk. The cracking of her heels. Seeing the mud-splattered brown shoe lying on its side just beyond the hedge's ragged corner.

"Malcolm," she whispered loudly, ran forward and

began to kneel.

The kneeling to a fall.

The fall to a scream.

There was the shoe, and the foot, and nothing else but the blood.

gliding

Voices in a distant corridor intruding upon a dream; respectful, awkward, fluttering into silence when she stirred and tossed her head from side to side on the stiff pillow. She sat up abruptly, one hand automatically gripping the sheet to her chest. The other darted to her lips, which trembled coldly against her fingers. The light was dim, and a figure moved from the shaded corner swiftly, stopping at the wooden footboard and smiling at her warmly.

"Sam," Vince said, "I thought you were snubbing me." His accent was Harvard thick, his hair Neapolitan black and luxuriantly thick; a rake is what her uncle had called him, and Vince had laughed at the telling.

Her breathing came in quick shallow gasps, but she managed a smile in return as bravely as she could. An image formed . . . she thrust it back. And as her vision cleared and she glanced toward the window, she realized it was afternoon, not evening: there was harsh sunlight on King Street, and she was back in the hospital, not in her home. The bed had been cranked up to a forty-five-degree angle, and when she slumped back to the pillow Vince remained in sight.

"You all right, kiddo?"

She passed a hand wearily over her forehead. "I'm beginning to feel like a character lost in those Gothics Angie reads," she said.

He shrugged shoulders that were a shadow too broad for the size of his torso, the size of his head. Then he punched impatiently at the unruly dark shock that hung stubbornly over his brow.

"How . . . have you been waiting here long?"

"Just a few minutes," he said, as though the time didn't matter. "Nurse Jones, or whatever her name is, said you hadn't been given anything for sleeping so I thought I might as well stick around for a while. You know how it is." He moved to sit on the edge of the mattress, her left leg shifting to give him room, the grace that was his hallmark giving her the impression he had hardly moved at all. He took her hand in his, lightly, without possession. "You've got us all worried, you know. The paperhanger even stopped threatening us until we knew how you were."

An image . . .

"Lord, do I look that bad?" She had aimed for a jest, knew she had fallen far short.

Vince grinned a denial. "Have the cops been bothering you? The rubber hose, third degree and all that?"

She accepted the diversion gratefully. "Hancock, bless his soul, came in the . . . the next day. And the day they brought me back. He's all right," she added quickly when Vince scowled. "He knows how hard something like this can be."

"Craig wants me to be sure, you know."

"I can take all the time I need," she said, imagining Reg's instructions. "Believe me, I know it. And I'll bet he's being so terribly efficient that Uncle Leonard is just busting for another stroke, trying to figure out how he can ease me back into the kitchen without ruining his reputation. Am I right, or am I right?"

He grinned, laughed, the intimacy of coworkers united against an enemy too clumsy and blatant to be even marginally threatening. It was, she understood, part of the curse of her sex: Leonard England owned the firm, and though he had never officially planted a title on either her or Craig, it was she who had taken over as the office's manager. For anyone else but Craig, however, her position would have been abundantly clear. He would not accept it, unfortunately, or was too dense to see it. A fiction. The others didn't mind. When trouble arose, they asked Samantha anyway.

"It's a sad thing to behold, Sam. The place is in a shambles." He stared at a point just over her head. "I don't think poor old Reg realized just how much you knew that wasn't written down. Like . . . well, young Toal came in day before yesterday, and Reg forgot that the man abhors smoking. After Reg dumped his second cigar, Toal picked up a magazine and cleared the air with it, and walked out without a word. I think Reg was ready to cry." The grin broadened and he leaned closer. "If you were smart, Sam, you'd get dear Uncle to sign it all over to you now, before Reg ruins us."

"I can't," she said softly. "He's really rather good."

"Yeah. I know. And surprising, sometimes."

She lifted an eyebrow.

"The day you came in, the first time, I suggested we think about taking another trip to the zoo. Great fun, silly as hell, and would you believe he and Danny were on the same side for a change? Boy, did I get lectures about animals in cages!"

Silly, she thought; that's what Reg needs—to be silly once in a while. He was the only one who hadn't taken that first trip.

A tall man in white came to the open door. Vince rose immediately and backed away.

"Samantha," Dave Greshton said. He hurried in with a smile, swiped the sidetable with his hip and had to lunge for the water pitcher before it struck the floor. As it was, his shoes were drenched.

"And you're supposed to be my doctor," she said, just loud enough for him to hear.

"Afternoon, Bartelle," the doctor said, his nod almost curt. "Must be nice not having to stick around the office all day."

"Just paying a call on my broker," Vince said briskly. "Can't have my investments following the weight of the world, you know. Besides, I want to be sure I'm in all the right companies when we take on the paperhanger. The way I see it, we'll be over there in a couple of years, and I'll be as rich as some doctors I know."

"That isn't funny," Greshton said. "And the man does have a name, Mr. Bartelle."

"Lord," Vince said, an anguished look to Sam. "Does Spike Jones know that? It'll kill him, you know."

"Bartelle . . . !"

Sam cleared her throat loudly. She supposed it should have been something of a pleasure to watch the two men sparring, presumably to impress her, but right now she wasn't in the mood.

Greshton, fussing with her wrist and the stethoscope around his neck, didn't hear her. Vince, however, glanced dramatically at the ceiling, then pulled a silver watch from his waistcoat pocket and frowned as though he had forgotten how to tell time. "Damn," he said.

"Hey, got to run, Sam, or poor Reg will have a stroke. Angie might be around tonight, depending on if she can get out of the clutches of that sailor she's been seeing; I half expect her to answer the phone with an 'Ahoy' instead of 'Hello.'

"Oh, and Danny said he would drop by your place, just to give it a check. Nice kid, that. Angie says he's gotten into the shed in back and even raked the lawn. Ten to one he'll join the Army once summer is over, though. He has dreams of keeping Europe in its place." When she grinned and winked, he blew her a kiss and was gone.

Greshton kept his silence. Continuing his fussing, he moved on to her blood pressure, her reflexes, her eyes and ears, and then to a thermometer before she snatched at his wrist and yanked his face close to hers. "If you don't tell me what's going on outside, David, I swear to God I'm going to check myself out."

"Now, Samantha—"

"Bullshit."

"Please, Samantha! I really think I'm doing the right thing, don't you?"

She didn't, not anymore, though she understood well and sympathized with his reticence. However, unless she was prepared to carry the swooning female role to its nauseating extreme, she knew she was going to have to begin taking hold before she was smothered by good intentions. Not, she told herself quickly, that she was ashamed of what she had done; it was not the average stock- and bond broker who came home at night to find a severed foot on the lawn, a foot that belonged to a man she might have been able to love. Angie Killough, who was the office receptionist and lived with her parents a block over from Sam's, had stayed with her those first two nights and had endured the aftermath of all those nightmares: the parade of beasts, of spectres, of demons and *things*, all of which tried to account for the death of the man.

On the second day, Angie had persuaded her to check into the hospital for a night under Greshton's care. One night. Free. A night of sheet lightning, but empty of dreams. Greshton had talked with her for over two hours, not minimizing the atrocity but cushioning the effect. The evening she returned home, however, the dreams had returned, this time of madmen who lived in the hills and were evilly chuckling experts at mutilations and horrors. She had made it through work, but barely. Later, she had been unable to bring herself to leave the sidewalk in front of the house until Danny, who had dogged her like a worried shadow, took a spade from the tool shed and turned over the earth where the grass had been trampled, shredded, and stained.

Tom Hancock had called on her that evening. Just thirty, he looked more like twenty, and when he folded his note pad back into his jacket pocket he smiled ruefully at her, brushing a hand almost apologetically through his close-cut blond hair.

"That's all you remember?"

She had nodded, not wanting to speak.

"Yeah," he said, his understanding clear. "Well, Miss England, there's nothing much else I can tell you now. From those drag marks we figure he was pulled into the woods. And that's about it. We haven't been able to find anything else. Nothing at his place, nothing around your house. I'd be less than honest if I told you we had a strong lead."

"You look tired," she said suddenly.

His smile was weary. "No kidding. It's the season, I guess." When she had frowned her puzzlement, he leaned back and sighed. "Spring, you know? We get calls all night. Girls staying out to all hours in the park, their folks think they're missing or worse. High school guys rodding around the streets, they ain't got anything better to do. Dogs and cats running away like they're expecting another Flood. And now this thing. Crazy. My dad, he was a cop up to Maine, he said I should get some small-town experience, then cut out for Boston or New York." The smile became a grin. "If it's like this down there, Miss England, I think I'll head back north."

She had folded her hands tightly in her lap. "Then . . . then you don't know if the . . . if the killer is a person or an animal."

"No, ma'am. Weather like this—hot as hell one day, cold like winter the next—there's no telling what it's doing to some people. Or some animals. I'm sorry, Miss England, but . . ." And he'd shrugged.

When he'd left her, she had a glass of wine to help her sleep.

And when the dreams came again—fiercer, more vivid—she had called Greshton for fear of retreating. It had been a precaution, nothing more. She did not believe she was losing her mind, but neither was she able to make the man understand that the house was . . . that it had somehow become too close, too small, far too small for the nighttrips her mind was taking. So she allowed herself to be watched, monitored, coddled, be-wombed. Three days away from the world, and now she was ready to smash through the window for a breath of fresh air instead of the slow-swirling blanket that was pushed by the ceiling's fan.

Greshton freed his wrist and started to crank down the bed, paused when he saw the look on her face.

"Samantha," he said with professional tolerance, "you have to get some sleep."

"For god's sake, David, I didn't have an operation, you know. And I'm getting a healthy crop of bedsores on my ass—"

"Samantha!"

"Oh, hell, David, will you please stop playing the role?" A moment for him to lick at his wounds with a contrition that almost sickened her. "David, I want to see Officer Hancock again."

"Why?"

She closed her eyes slowly. "Because," she said, drawing out the word as though he were a child backward and trying, "I want to know if they've been able to find out anything more, that's why. Really, is that so difficult for you to understand?"

Greshton stared at her for a long second, one finger stroking his chin thoughtfully. "It might upset you, Samantha."

"I'm a big girl, David."

"You'll forgive me for saying so, but you didn't act like one a couple of days ago."

She pushed at the mattress to sit herself more upright. "You didn't see what I saw, *Doctor*."

"Well . . ."

"If I hadn't turned a hair, you would have thought I was crazy, right?"

"I don't know Samantha. I don't know if I—"

"David, please."

He looked at her with cautious concern, permitting a trace of a smile to work finally at his bloodless lips. Then, with a sigh that was more noise than release, he sat heavily on the bed and slapped his hands on his legs. "Okay. What do you want to know?"

She grinned. "Good lord, the man's a gossip."

But there was little he told her that she did not already know, little he could add to the speculation in the Station as to the identity of Malcolm's killer. No weapons had been found, no enemies uncovered, no animals discovered; it was even impossible to tell if the foot had been hacked or chewed off because of the apparently violent manner in which it had been severed. Though the police were still searching, it was Hancock's private theory that if the rest of the man's body was going to be found at all, it would be somewhere in the woods. Deep, and accidentally. A stumbling over a mutilated form by someone bent on looking for something far more innocent.

And though there had been a hunt through the forest, it was more than likely that the killer, no matter who or what it had been, was already long gone.

"Satisfied?"

"I suppose."

"You want me to get you a book?"

"Please," she said. "I can't count the holes in the ceiling anymore."

He laughed and was gone. Reg called her during dinner, and she was barely able to conceal her surprise, and her guilt, at his genuine condolences. Vince called. Angie dropped by.

Not a word from her uncle; but, unlike Malcolm, he was still dying.

And that night, when the corridors were still, the lights hushed, the window open from the bottom and admitting the darkside chorus of treefrogs and nightbirds, she lay in a small pool of light and waited for her medication to start working. Unafraid, now; the dreams had been vanquished.

She tried to think, but there was little to think about. David had made it abundantly clear that her apprehension over the house was a referral from her work; the economy was finally stirring—not spectacularly, but stronger—and her natural impatience to get on with it was giving her a mild case of claustrophobia, and a strong one of intolerance. The house was confining, squeezing, because there was no work there to challenge her, not the kind of work she enjoyed, not the dealing or the probing or the ferreting of financial hints that would reinstate in her clients a faith in the system. Oxrun had not been severely affected by the Depression; those who had their wealth to hand had not been foolish enough to plunge into the market as deeply as those who had had much more to lose—and did. Even the Station's middle class had had more sense. Oxrun, as always, took care of its own.

It was explained to her, then, that this knowledge would enable her to cope—not only with Malcolm's death, but also with her own life.

Perhaps, she thought; maybe.

But she had been just as impatient last year, and no fears had assailed her.

She shrugged, and she slept, and the following morning she could no longer stand it. She dressed over the nurse's mild objections, argued lightly with Greshton, and kissed him once before she left. There was no one to accompany her, and she was glad; she did not mind a moment on her own, in the air, to confront the house.

She needed to know if David had been right.

And when she saw it, she could not help a small laugh and a delighted smile. Danny had raked and mowed the lawn to new-green perfection, washed the windows, trimmed and weeded the flower bed on the house's north side, and had somehow contrived to make the privet look amazingly like a hedge instead of a bed-raggled copse in the middle of some dark moor. The air was lightly chilled, the sun no longer harsh, and the stabs of apprehension she expected did not reach her. The brown shingles were welcoming instead of seeming glum, and she thought she spotted a stirring in the jay's nest in the elm by the porch.

The inside had been aired and dusted.

The icebox was filled.

And Angie had left a cold casserole on the kitchen's grey-and-blue Formica table.

She nearly wept, and would have done so had she not been suddenly taken with the idea that the most extravagant thing she could do to celebrate her home-coming was take a shower. She raced immediately up the stairs, stripped, and turned on the water, listening contentedly to the thrumming, watching the steam, feeling the flesh around her small breasts and slightly pudgy stomach, her upper arms and thighs, tighten in anticipation.

It was heaven, and she deserved it.

She grabbed the showercap and settled it over her hair. Then mouthed *doxy* when she caught her re-flection in the mirror just before it fogged over; and she laughed, loudly and cleanly, exploding into fits of giggling over the next several hours . . . until she was in bed and the moon threw slats of silver over the blanket that covered her.

The moon.

She turned away from it, waiting, her breath held lightly, her right hand gripping the end of her pillow while her left tucked itself between her knees, knees that were drawn protectively toward her chest. Away from the window, toward the door.

The moon.

The quiet.

Waiting, and listening.

But the slow crushing tension was apparently gone.

Then she rolled onto her back and laced her fingers behind her head, thinking that somehow she should weep again for Malcolm, should at least rekindle the rage that had come with his dying.

And that too was gone, the weeping and the ranting.

He had been a friend, not a lover, and not even from the Station. There was sorrow, and a slight drifting, and she thought before sleeping that Vince would understand.

the muted hush of

An argument in the outer office, finally driving her to slap an angry hand on her desk and rise, kicking back her chair and stalking to the door. She hesitated, brushed a hand down the front of her ruffled, cream satin blouse, and tried to bring herself calm. It was the season, she told herself, thinking of poor Hancock and his chasing of runaway pets; to be charitable, it was the season.

The weather over the past two weeks had been no less erratic, but the trees had finally covered themselves in a soft haze of new green, the park was so brightly new it hurt the eyes, and the last taunts of winter had faded into nights that were just warm and languid enough for memories of years past and kisses shared and walks taken and loves begun. The season. When the lofty pronouncements of poets and romantics were distilled into the inarguable fact that everyone was crazy.

Including herself.

She opened the door, then, and winced.

The room was large, nearly sixty feet to the front where the plate-glass window was quartered by gleaming white curtains that now kept the westering sun from turning the place into a furnace in spite of the elms outside that filtered the light. The walls were wainscoted in dark pine, the ceiling white and high, the floor carpeted in floral oriental. By the entrance, and separated by a low mahogany table neatly stacked with newspapers and magazines, were high-backed brown leather club chairs. Farther inward was Angie's walnut reception desk, a tangle of pink-faced note slips and tall-cradled telephones that were somewhere made rational by the tolerance of her smile. A few paces more to a partition of ebony chin-high and translucent, beyond which was a double row of similarly partitioned desks—vacationing John Nesbitt on the left, an empty one on the right; Vince behind Nesbitt, Reg Craig on the other side of the aisle. In the back wall, three doors—Sam's on the right, her uncle's, and a brass-plated, decorous entrance to a restroom as large as the one she had at home.

Craig was standing in the center aisle, leaning over

Vince's desk and hissing at him like, she thought, an aroused viper pit.

"And furthermore," he was saying, "I do not give a sweet goddamn what you or—" He stopped at a furtive gesture from Bartelle, looked over his shoulder and strained a grin. "Oh. Hello, Samantha."

Her own grin was genuine, made more so when she saw Danny pop up from behind the front partition and stick out his tongue at Craig's blind side. The boy was slender, not quite twenty, given constantly to collarless shirts and patternless sweaters with raglan sleeves. Chewing gum bulged his left cheek, a pencil balanced rakishly behind his right ear. His hair was thick and dark brown, parted down the middle and combed back so it almost fanned out when it reached his ears. His skin was curiously dusky, and his eyes were slightly hooded, yet he seemed to Sam to be more Saxon than Mediterranean. He stuck out his tongue again, then mimed extreme agony when Angie pinched him.

"Gentlemen," Sam said, exaggerating a tone of exhausted impatience, "which one of you has bollixed a portfolio this time."

"Neither," said Vince, rocking back in his swivel chair and snapping a wooden match against his center drawer. "Reg here seems to think that FDR has been given a mandate to rule by divine right. After suggesting the possible virtues of Norman Thomas, I, on the other hand, have suggested with all the diplomacy I can muster that the man is nothing more than an imperialist and budding two-bit emperor. I mean really, Samantha —three terms? God, even Jefferson was satisfied with two."

Craig, whose white linen suit nearly matched the

blinding glare of the front curtains, shot his cuffs and glared at an original Currier & Ives on the wall above Bartelle's head. "I merely said that he will not, under any circumstances, allow us to fall for German entrapment again."

"Crap," Vince said, with a disarming smile.

Sam put a hand to her hair, pushed at it, gripped lightly the back of her neck. "Really, do we have to go through all that again? Doesn't anyone here but me have any work to do?"

"The market's closed," Vince said with a glance to his watch.

"Marvelous. Do you think we should close down then?"

He looked to his blotter and touched at a paper. Reg toyed with his bow tie, then pulled a pen from his jacket pocket and turned around to his desk. At that moment, Danny came rushing up the aisle and grabbed for the pen.

"Hey!" Reg said, pulling his hand away.

"It's mine," said the boy, scowling, hands suddenly fisted at his sides.

"I'm afraid it isn't," Reg told him stiffly. He held it close to Danny's eyes. "You can see my initials engraved there. In gold, in case you did not know what all the yellow was."

"Well . . . it looked like mine."

Sam immediately stepped between them, one hand on Reg's shoulder. "Danny," she said softly.

The boy shoved his hands into his pockets and scuffed a worn shoe over the carpet. "Well . . ."

"Danny," she repeated, prompting now and smiling.

"I'm sorry," he muttered.

"No harm done," Reg said expansively, suddenly noting Sam's hand on his shoulder and slipping his own around her wrist. It was a gesture completely unconscious, more paternal than affectionate, but she could not help noticing the abrupt narrowing of the boy's eyes and the rigid way Vince sat up and stared across the room. The moment lasted no longer than it took her to recognize it and move deftly away. But she was startled, and somewhat flattered, that a simple gesture from someone like Reg Craig could produce such an intense reaction.

Maybe, she thought, she should take hospital breaks more often.

She almost laughed then, cleared her throat instead and squinted at the wall clock by her door. Problems, she realized; there could be problems here if I don't watch out. Danny, for whatever reasons, was becoming increasingly possessive of late; and Vince . . . well, she did not want him thinking that Reg was something he wasn't. And that idea amused her, too, when she realized that it mattered. Had mattered, in fact, even while Malcolm was alive and both young man and older were attempting to discourage her from seeing him. Vince and Daniel. This time she did grin.

"Listen," she said, "if you all are going to debate the problems of the world, would you mind at least keeping it down to a dull roar? I have a lot of paperwork to catch up on yet, and I really don't feel like taking anything home tonight."

"Lord save the poor working girl," Vince said.

"Spring fever," Reg muttered, and slumped down in his chair.

"Miss England," Danny said then, staring down at

his shoes almost buried by his trousers' cuffs, "I got a . . . a friend's car tonight. It's a LaSalle. It's a red one." He looked up. Smiled. "Cary Grant's over to Harley. With Betsy Drake, I think."

She almost sputtered, tried not to scowl when she caught Vince's amused expression, and she would have been curt had she not also seen Reg's puff-chested condescension. "No," she said gently, though she managed to keep her smile. "I'm really not up to it now. But thanks for asking."

Danny shrugged. "That's all right. Shaw's going to be in Hartford, anyway. I guess I'd rather dance." Immediately, he reached down for Bartelle's wastebasket and carried it off, through the door that led into the alley.

"Pup," Reg said, poking at the folders on his blotter. "Insolent. Don't know why you hired him, Samantha."

She lay a hand carefully atop his, her expression clear enough to make him leave his work alone. Then she smiled sweetly at him. "As I recall, Reginald, my dear, it was you who took him on. I remember further that you felt sorry for him, or words to that effect."

"He's still a pup," the man said sourly. "Wanders around town all the time, never goes home . . . wouldn't be surprised if he's been picking up all those dogs and selling them in New York. Big black market in that sort of thing, you know." He looked away from Sam's astonishment and rose, forcing her back. "He'll be drafted anyway, you'll see. The Army will be good for him. Toughen him up. He's . . . too pretty, if you know what I mean."

She did not trust herself to reply. She had known Reg for nearly fifteen years, and had never heard him raise his voice except in an argument over politics; nor had she ever seen him struggling quite so hard for control. It puzzled her because she didn't know why a boy, an office boy, should affect him so. Perhaps, she thought, he was mad because Danny had had the nerve to ask her out in front of him, and though she knew he was interested in her he had never once made what she could recognize as anything close to an advance. Unless the hand at her waist . . .

"It's a crush," Vince said as Reg headed back for the restroom.

"What?" Reg turned slowly.

"A crush, man. Come on, Reg, you know what that is. The boy's in love with every woman on the street. You should see him at work in the park sometime. He picks out a chick and follows her everywhere until she either tells him to get lost or . . ." He spread his hands and grinned.

"Oh. And I suppose you, Bartelle, don't have to stoop to such tactics."

Vince waved his cigarette in the air, drew on it, watched the smoke writhe toward Craig's paunch. "I manage, old man, I manage."

Reg snorted his disgust and stalked into the restroom, the door closing heavily, just this side of a slam.

"Good lord," Sam said. "What's gotten into him?"

"Asta."

She blinked, slowly. "We were talking about Reg, not William Powell."

He stubbed out his cigarette, pulled a copy of the *Station Herald* from his desk and tapped at a small article near the bottom of the front page. She read it quickly, an announcement that the Harley and Oxrun

Station police forces were setting up a joint investigative team whose sole function would be to smash the apparent petnapping ring that was terrorizing the two communities.

"Terrorizing?" she said.

"Sam, you were born and raised here. You've been in homes where people think money is the reward you get for opening your eyes in the morning. And you've seen their pets. Pampered, spoiled, loved as though they were human, and worth, at times, in the thousands. How would you feel if it up and went on you?"

"All right, but what does that have to do with—" She stopped. "Oh."

"Yeah," he said. "Last night. He and whatever he calls it, the terrier, were in the park. It took off on him, and he hasn't seen it since."

She put a hand to her forehead. "Brother. Then—"

A sudden clatter of trash cans in the alley interrupted her. Danny returned to drop the wastebasket in its place. He said nothing to them, only walked briskly down the aisle toward the front, pausing just long enough to pinch Angie's back before grabbing up a broom and leaving. A moment later she could see him swiping viciously at the pavement in front of the building.

The ticker tape in her office chimed to life, chattered, and stilled.

"Do you think he heard?" she said without looking away.

"He'd be deaf if he didn't."

"Oh, dear."

"Mother to the world," he said gently. "When are you ever going to learn to relax. Better yet, throw yourself into my arms and tell me you're going to Southampton with me."

"I thought you already had a . . . companion."

"I could get a headache."

"You could get fired."

"Is that a hint or an answer?"

She grinned at him. "You're the expert. You figure it out." Then she returned to her desk, leaving the door open. She heard nothing while she worked for the next hour, nothing when she leaned back and stared blindly at the ceiling. It was time, she thought, something was done about Danny. It had been fun in the beginning, toying with him and knowing neither took the other very seriously. But today was the first time he'd ever broached the subject of an evening together. That worried her. It was wrong. And she had no intention of encouraging him if it meant his feelings would be hurt no matter how pleasant her rejection.

It was wrong, but her face sharpened suddenly into a mischievous mask.

On the other hand, accepting one of his proposals would certainly put him back into the pleasant mood he'd been in over the past two weeks; not to mention the apoplexy it would give Reg and the blow it would be to Vince's ever so carefully manicured Harvard poise.

She put a hand to her mouth to muffle a laugh, renewed her attack on the portfolio and somehow managed to find that maddeningly lost key just before she realized she was alone in the office. She sighed and stretched, looking out through her door to the now-closed curtains, the dim lights beyond as Oxrun closed down for the night. The desks and partitions were formless and dark, reminding her for no reason of a painting she had seen, of a nightscape, a desert, rocks and buttes just after sunset. Though the sky was brilliant with the day's afterglow, everything else had been done in shades of black.

An automobile backfired to accentuate the silence.

She wondered as she gathered her things together if she should call Herb's Taxi and ride out beyond the park to see her uncle. She was due for a visit, but she did not want the depression. He barely knew her, barely spoke unless the question was repeated three or four times. A year ago, two, she had wept each time she left; now, without any guilt, she hoped that his doctors would either give him his miracle and bring him back, or let him die. She would miss him. But her mourning was done.

No. Not tonight. Tonight she would take Vince's advice: she would relax and read and listen to the radio and get to bed early before her weariness opened the gates for the dreams.

She checked the side door's lock, fussed a bit with Angie's desk and left.

Walked.

Thought May was the month for poets and lovers, and wondered if Byron or Shelley had had their best work done before the full heat of summer put a lid on simple dreaming.

At the police station, Tom Hancock was standing at the curb with two of his partners. They nodded to her as she passed, but she gave Tom a smile he took for himself. She almost stopped then to ask if he knew more about Malcolm, knew without asking he would tell her if he did.

And it was a measure of her mood that the thought

did not slow her. It was too pleasant an evening and her step too light. Even the blandness of her dinner did not spoil her spring fever, and she was grinning still after washing the dishes, stacking them to air dry, wiping counter and table and folding the striped towel to hang over a chair. When she glanced at her watch she realized she'd missed the news, shrugged because she'd no desire tonight to hear about the fighting. It was too far away. Like sitting in the high balcony's last row and watching a vague tragedy about people she didn't know.

Tomorrow, she told herself; I'll think about it tomorrow.

She lay a palm over the lightswitch by the hall door, pressed and let the room accept its ration of night.

And froze as though someone had nudged a blade against her spine.

The house was completely dark, a chill already seeping across the floorboards to her ankles. Slowly, she glanced over her right shoulder toward the back door. She had taken the blue curtains down the day before to clean them, and the six small panes were squares of suspended black ice that shimmered suddenly when an abrupt darting wind richocheted off the house. She turned, and listened, as her arm dropped to her side.

A *whisper*soft sound, lingering, trailing, an impression of weight dragged across new moist grass.

She eased away from the wall, and with one arm slightly out to maintain her balance walked off her heels around the dark table.

*Whisper*soft. Circling.

She kicked a chair and stiffened.

*Whisper*soft. Fading.

With hands cupped and cold around her eyes she

pressed her forehead against a pane and squinted, seeing nothing in the dark but the dim impatience of leaves twisting away from the wind.

She strained, and heard nothing.

Closed her fingers around the knob and opened the door.

The cold made her gasp, and she hugged herself tightly as she stepped out onto the narrow back stoop. The woodland on the left seemed closer and looming, the trees around the tool shed trembling and distant. Clouds butted the moon. The single window in the shed caught some of the light and winked at her, leering, before the light died. Her blouse was loose and was no protection, the hair that swept back from her face in set curl-rolls tugged at her face until she was grimacing.

A dog, she thought then, or that damned tom of Kramer's.

It was a good enough answer that was no answer at all, and she backed inside to close the door quickly, hurrying into the hallway to stop at the telephone table at the foot of the stairs. Her teeth clicked together hard, and she stamped a foot to bring her warmth. But by the time the shuddering and the stamping was done she had decided there was no reason to call the police; and if she called anyone else they would think of Dave Greshton and the hospital on King and they would calm her and voice-smile and not believe her at all.

Believe what? she asked herself then. I heard a noise. A dog or a cat. *The dogs were all gone.* A dog or a cat hunting garbage to root through.

"Ridiculous," she said, and was inordinately pleased at the calm in her voice. Then, whispering: "Please don't let it come back."

She walked into the living room and switched on a standing lamp, dropped into her favorite armchair and plucked a *Collier's* from the cranberry-scoop magazine rack at her side. She crossed her legs at the knee. Again, the other way. Tugged at a stray curl. Pulled at her nose. Dropped the magazine to the carpet and reached for the newspaper before realizing she hadn't stopped to pick one up.

"Samantha," she warned herself.

She stared at the Emerson across the room, but it seemed suddenly too large, the speaker grilles in an arc around the central dial gaping mouths that spewed out the dark.

"Damnit!"

None of this would have happened if it hadn't been for Vince and Reg. Their arguments in the office, the tensions they created with Danny in the center, all of it flooding her senses until they were numb. It was false, thinking she had managed to joke her way through the afternoon. She had done nothing but aggravate the situation. Reg. Vince. Danny. The stoic, the rake, the boy. She put fingers to her cheeks and rubbed them softly, pushed her hand back through her hair and felt the pins dislodge. It was their fault; she'd been doing fine until today.

Now . . . now, suddenly, she needed a voice.

She pushed herself out of the chair and walked back into the hall, grabbed the heavy black receiver and gave the operator a number. Her foot tapped impatiently. She kept her back firm to the kitchen.

"Hello?"

Damn, she thought, and could not understand how she'd gotten Reg.

"Reg, it's Samantha."

There was a pause she could not read, but when he spoke again his voice was soft.

"Samantha, for heaven's sake. To what do I owe the pleasure?"

Flustered, still muttering under her breath at her idiocy, she managed to blunder through something about the office and her work. Then she cut herself off and could sense him frowning.

"Samantha, are you all right?" Now the voice was deep. Paternal. She felt again the hand on her waist and she sighed, loudly.

"I'm fine, Reg," she said. "Look, this is going to sound awfully silly, but I really wasn't calling you."

"Ah," he said, as though he understood.

"I mean, I gave the wrong number to the operator. I was calling someone else."

"Indeed." A pause. "A couple of weeks ago I was trying to get hold of my mother in Greenwich. I ended up with the local police. I felt like a complete fool, believe me, calling the desk sergeant 'Mother.' "

She twisted the wire in her left hand, and smiled. "Thanks, Reg."

He laughed. "Hey, wait a minute, Samantha, I didn't mean it that way."

"I know. I was just teasing."

Explain, she thought; the man has no imagination. She remembered the sound and wished she were the same.

"But listen, Samantha, as long as you're on the line, would you mind telling me what . . ."

She frowned. "Reg? Reg, are you there?"

"Yes," he said, seemingly distracted. "Yes, of

course. There was something . . . Samantha, would you mind hanging on for a minute? I think there's someone on the porch. Maybe he's found Asta. Would you mind?''

She nodded, then blurted a "go ahead" though she knew he had already left her. Nice, she thought; very nice, Sam. One lousy dog taking a shortcut has galloped you into instant senility.

She was still chiding herself half-heartedly, her gaze drifting around the hallway, when she heard the shout. A man's shout, full-voiced and high. A shout that became a scream, a scream sliced abruptly into silence.

"Reg?"

*Whisper*soft.

"Reg!"

The protestation of floorboards as something dragged over them.

ghosts slipping over

The line breaking into a shrill wail that made her snap the receiver away from her ear. She stared at it, gaping, her lips working at words that would not come, while her breath came in quick, shallow bursts. The wailing died. She jabbed at the cradle frantically until the operator returned, snapped out Reg's address and a demand for the police, and was in her coat and out the front door before there was a response.

She would not let herself think, would not let herself imagine.

It wasn't until she had swerved around the corner and was racing up King Street that she realized she hadn't put on her shoes, that pebbles and twigs were digging into her soles. But she did not falter; instead, she welcomed them, and their swift stabs of pain: they kept her mind off the scream, off the sounds and the silence she had heard when the scream had died.

Another right turn and she was on Fox Road, slowing now as she approached the woodland wall four blocks distant. Stopping for a moment when she saw the cascade of light from Craig's small home across the way, mirrored by those of his neighbors to either side. She stepped off the curb, arms folded over her stomach, hands gripping her elbows. Now that she was here she didn't know what to do, could not bring herself to search the lawns for signs of— She froze, then, when a patrol car rushed past her and halted nose in to the curb. Four men scattered from the vehicle instantly, the last Tom Hancock, who turned and waited for her. Another car split them, another quartet, and floodlights from the roof turned the area a flat, dead white.

"You move fast," Hancock said when she was close enough to hear.

"I . . ." She couldn't. Her eyes would not move away from the front stoop, from the open door. Dimly she heard voices as people filtered onto their lawns, speculating and calling, driving back the night with ill-timed jokes and friendly jibes at the police.

A small, heavyset woman in a quilted bathrobe and furry pink mules came up to Hancock and pulled at his arm urgently. "The bums," she said, voice cracking. Hancock gave her his best professional smile. "The bums," she said again, jutting her chin toward the woods. Another woman joined her; they could have been sisters. "They come around at night, knocking over garbage cans, breaking windows, drunk all the time on that hooch they make by the tracks. You find them, Officer, you find your man.''

"Have you seen any of them tonight?" he asked.

The first woman shook her head. "Heard them, though. They must have stripped that poor man's house, from the sounds of it.''

"How do you figure, Mrs. . . .''

"Ferguson," she said. "Mrs. Howard Ferguson. I heard them. Yep, I heard them. Sounded like they was dragging a piano off, for god's sake.''

Sam shuddered and looked away.

*Whisper*soft.

Hancock put an arm around the woman's shoulders and thanked her as he led her back to her group of friends, who surrounded her quickly, chattering while their glances kept bouncing off Sam.

"Interesting," the policeman said, and said it again when Sam told him about her conversation with Reg, the conversation and the interruption. She was about to ask him angrily if that was all he could say when a sudden shift of bodies toward the woods forestalled her, a movement accompanied by a man's summoning call. Hancock instructed her to stay where she was and ran off. She obeyed him. She didn't want to know what they had discovered, sensing nevertheless that it would be something like Malcolm.

She waited alone in the middle of the street, moving only when an ambulance squealed around the corner and headed for the concentration of lights at the block's end. Roadblocks were being set up, and the black air was chopped by darting spotlights that froze the trees against themselves and made all movement seem jerky and uncoordinated. She rubbed the bottom of one foot against her leg, had shifted to the other when Hancock returned and asked if she wouldn't mind riding with him back to the station; just long enough, he assured her gently, to dictate a statement. And while she was there, sitting at his desk behind the low wooden railing, she overheard two patrolmen talking as they came in, one of them threatening not very seriously to resign if "this damned stuff kept up," the other insisting that the lower half of Craig's body had not been cut off with an ax, but bitten at and torn.

Hancock barely got her into the restroom before she threw up.

And when it was done, her face wiped dry with paper towels and her hair shoved clumsily and uncaringly back into place, she saw Vince waiting for her outside. She didn't care what Hancock or the others thought; she dropped into his surprised embrace and allowed herself to weep, to shudder at the ice that had replaced her blood, to let him drive her home and sit with her in the parlour while she tried to make some sense of Reg's killing.

"It's me," she said at one point, and felt him stiffen briefly. Pushing herself away and into the corner of the couch, she wiped an already damp handkerchief over her face. "I mean, first Mal and now Reg. I knew them, Vince, I knew them."

"So did I," he said softly. He was in shirtsleeves and dark trousers, his hair tousled and face lined as he'd gotten out of bed to come to her. "So did a lot of people, for that matter."

"Well, I suppose . . . but they were in love with me."

A single lamp cast tasseled shadows over the floor. He stared at them and brushed both hands through his hair. "There are others," he said.

A walnut Seth Thomas perched on the radio chimed the half hour.

"Maybe I'm a jinx," she whispered.

"Sure. And Shirley Temple's a hooker."

"I mean it, Vince," she said, straightening as the notion took hold, found sense, if not reason. "Look, suppose somebody wants me so badly that he's willing to kill for it. Kind of like getting rid of the opposition."

"Good God," he said, barely hiding his disgust, "you go to too many movies, for crying out loud." He yanked a crumpled pack of cigarettes from his breast pocket and offered her one. She shook her head, and he took it for himself, blowing the smoke toward the ceiling and glaring at it. "That's Ellery Queen stuff, Sam. Come on, you're smarter than that. Besides . . ." He sighed. "You want me to give a call to Dave?"

Her voice was cold: "Why?"

He smiled. "It's not because I think you're cracking up, m'dear. I meant, to get a sedative from him. You're not going to get much sleep, you know."

That much was true. But if he were trying to force her off the subject, he had failed. Once lodged, the idea that there was someone out there who was willing to do . . . to mutilate in order to isolate her took root and would not be ignored. She attempted again to explain it to him, and again he scoffed, albeit gently.

"For the sake of argument, however," he said, easing back into his own corner and crossing his legs, "let's say that it's true. Who, then, are you thinking of? Danny? The kid is a born womanizer, you know that as well as I do. And the only person he really loves is himself. I was in on that little byplay with Reg at the office, remem-

ber? You saw what happened: the boy is too easily pro-
voked, and just as easily distracted."

"Maybe."

He laughed. "No maybes about it, Sam. He is still a
kid, a half-baked, slightly weird teenager who's looking
for a quick way to grow up. Although, if I do say so
myself, he is quite the chip off the old office block, as it
were." His laughter grew when she looked at him,
shocked. "Well, come on, Sam! Why not consider me?
You know . . ." He faltered. "Well, you know what I
think, Sam. But please don't take offense when I tell
you that I'm not about to risk the pleasures of the
electric chair just to win your favors. I do it my way, or
no way at all."

"Then . . . who?"

"Then nobody, for god's sake," he said sternly.
"Sam, for a broker you're one lousy plotter. It does
happen in real life, you know. People who know other
people die. They get killed. There is no connection,
Sam, only coincidence. Rotten, to be sure, but it's still
coincidence."

She wanted to believe him, wanted to agree, and
allowed him to think she did until he was unable to stifle
a yawn and she urged him out of the house. And once
alone, in the kitchen and standing in front of the stove,
she stared at the blue gas flame and prayed he was right.
Otherwise . . .

When she slept, just before dawn, there were dreams
of walking through the zoo, alone, at night. And in each
cage she passed there was a creature—lion, tiger, serpent, *something*—feeding on pieces of people she knew.
Yet she was not revolted; the screams that she heard
were the screams of the dying. It wasn't until she reached the last cage and the largest that she saw her own face

lacerated, her own chest devoured. Then she screamed. And then she woke up.

When she walked to the office, then, she found herself staring at faces. Round, oval, squared, florid, pasty, puffed, trying to see behind the mask to the world and through the eyes to the motivations behind. She found herself flinching whenever someone accidentally brushed against her, starting when a horn blared, shivering whenever she was forced through shadow. By the time she reached her desk her hands were trembling, and she could feel her heart working twice its normal pace to keep her from fainting. Foolish. It was all so damned foolish it made perfect sense. The only thing she didn't understand was the method.

By ten o'clock she had had enough. Her eyes weren't working, and her mind kept wandering. Since Danny hadn't come in and Angie seemed as nerve-shot as she—the same as after Malcolm, she thought, with a sigh almost relief—she closed the office down and went to the park to think. Sat near the pond and watched the ducks feeding, felt the sun crawl over her, the air chill toward twilight. Returned home saddened because during the whole time she hadn't seen one small child playing with a pet, realized that people had started walking their dogs in pairs, in groups, and she wondered if Tom had made any progress there.

And for some reason, that problem seemed as important as hers. Or minor, she thought when she took a look at herself before going to bed.

Vince called to bid her good night.

The zoo dream returned, longer and more vivid.

The *Station Herald* claimed there was a bear loose in the hills.

At the office she kept her door closed, wondering if it

was possible for an animal like that to be trained to kill.

By noon she was beginning to think she was playing Ingrid Bergman to someone's Charles Boyer; except that someone was obviously herself, and it was her own continuing reaction to Mal's death that was nudging her toward the edge.

She ate lunch by herself, but once done she opened the door and saw Vince on the telephone, Angie at the switchboard, Danny puttering up the aisle with a broom in his hand. Normal. The first shock was over and it was all perfectly normal. Even to the point of John Nesbitt calling in from the Cape, telling her his car had broken down and he would be a couple of days late getting back to work. Every year. Every . . . year. It was normal.

She leaned against the jamb and watched as Danny stopped by Vince's desk and began talking. She overheard fragments, enough to understand that the police had rousted the hobo camp near the tracks, had nearly a dozen of them at the station now for questioning. Danny suspected they were grasping at straws, and she was surprised when Vince snapped at him angrily, driving the boy back to his work. When he finally reached the back of the office she smiled and asked him in for a moment.

His hands immediately burrowed into his pockets, his gaze stayed on her desktop, everything about his stance readying for a scolding.

"Hey," she said lightly, "you're not fired, you know."

His grin was more relief than mirth. "I didn't mean to bother him. Thought he wanted to hear things, that's all."

"It's all right, Danny. He's probably overtired. He

was up late last night with me." Then she couldn't help a short laugh at his consternation. "He picked me up at the police station and took me home, Danny. I . . . well, Mr. Craig was on the phone with me when it happened."

Danny nodded his sympathy. "Yeah, I heard. That's terrible, Miss England, and I'm sorry. Things like that shouldn't happen to you." His face brightened suddenly. "You could have called me, you know. I would have helped you."

"Well, I appreciate the thought, Danny, really."

He looked away to the floor. "You don't have to be afraid of me."

"I'm not."

"I mean, I—"

"That," she said carefully, "is quite enough, don't you think?"

He nodded dejectedly, and she almost spoke to console him, decided against it and picked up a pencil instead to roll between her palms. "Tell me something, Danny. You're on the street a lot. Do you think those men they picked up—or one of them, anyway—had anything to do with . . . Mr. Craig?" She had tried to sound offhanded, but her voice nearly cracked and she had to clear her throat twice to prevent a coughing spasm. Dumb, she told herself; even Danny would be the first to agree.

"Oh, no," he said. He glanced over his shoulder, back again and leaned closer. "I mean, just look at—well, I mean, just look at it, Miss England. You'd have to be crazy to do something like that." He was nearly crouching now, his face masked conspiratorially. "I get around, you know? I read the paper this morning, that thing about the bears and I think it's right. People think there're too many houses and stuff out here, too many people, but in the spring some of them always come back. You ask the farmers out in the valley, they'll tell you. They usually keep away—the bears, I mean—but sometimes they like to take after the garbage, things like that. Take my word for it, Miss England, them cops going to find themselves a winter-mad bear once they get going.''

She stared at him blankly, just long enough to start a frown on her brow. Then, remembering her near-hysteria with Vince the other night, the article, and her search for the elusive "method" of killing, she said, "Amazing."

"Huh?"

She gestured at him vaguely. "Nothing. I was just thinking, Danny, just thinking. You know, sometimes people can really be dense, really stupid." She hesitated. "Danny, are you still planning to see Artie Shaw this weekend?"

His eyes widened and his chin sagged. "Holy cow, Miss—"

"Nonono," she said quickly, smiling and shaking her head. "I'm sorry, but I'm still not ready for you yet, Danny. But I know a man, a customer, and he's what you call a promoter, who just might be able to see to it you don't lack for space right at the bandstand."

Disappointment almost angrily bitter was replaced by something she could only label awe. "You mean it?" When she nodded he started for the door, stopped and looked back over his shoulder. "But what did I do?"

"Don't ask."

"Miss England, you don't have to tell me nothin' twice."

He ducked out laughing, and she had to restrain herself from blowing a kiss after him. From the mouths of babes, she thought. A bear. A stupid . . . bear. An animal is what her dreams had been trying to tell her, but she had been so caught up in her own egocentric theory that she'd blocked all reason out. The newspaper, Danny, and Vince had all been right. Coincidences and animals. And when she called Tom Hancock, she found out there'd been a hunting party in the hills since yesterday's dawn. It might also, he said, explain all those damned missing cats and dogs.

The nose on your face, she thought, is never quite so plain as you think it is.

Ten minutes after she rang off, Vince left behind a plea of a splitting headache. Angie was gone at the first stroke of five, and Danny was right behind her. Through the drawn curtains and the door's window shade, the glow from Centre Street's lights reminded her of the moonhaze that presaged a storm. "Last again," she muttered as she cleared her desk and reached for the cardigan on her office rack. It was getting to be a habit she would just as soon not perpetuate. Uncle Leonard and his business aside, she would rather not be saddled with the reputation of being all work and no play. Smiling ruefully, then, she paused on the threshold, looking out over the desks to the black wall of the first partition. Funny, but Vince hadn't asked her out since she'd returned from the hospital. Perhaps it was in deference to Mal's death, and perhaps she had put him off too strongly over the winter. Whatever the reason, she didn't like it and decided it was time to contrive a business lunch at the Inn . . .

. . . and heard the sound as clearly as she heard her breath catch in her throat.

thin ice clinging to black water, sighs slipping from the lips of dead men still dying

In the far corner by the front door, a shadow that seemed a blackshade darker than those around it. An exhalation, like slow sighing steam escaping from the radiators that humped against the walls.

*Whisper*soft.

She almost grabbed for her door to slam it shut, to lock herself in her office until someone came to find her. But her hand stayed, and she moved slowly toward Vince's desk, her feet shuffling over the carpet, her knees slightly bent as her left hand stretched out to sweep for obstacles that might betray her. She paused only once, thinking she would call out for an explanation, to tell the intruder she kept no money here and she would not call the police if he would only leave her alone. And at the same time she was amazed to realize she was more cautious than afraid, feeling as yet unthreatened by whoever was watching.

Her thumb brushed over the desk's corner. She stopped again, straining through the lightglow to the darkness at its side, seeing nothing now but pinpoints of color like static that refused to be dialed into sound.

She tilted her head; the shadow was there.

And now there was fear as the room filled with the steamnoise, the hissing, the steady patient waiting.

She glanced quickly to her left at the alley door and its bar latch. Plenty of time to reach it. And if she were quick enough she might be able to get to the street and grab someone to help her. She was known. Most of them out there knew her by sight if not by introduction, and they would know she wasn't a drinker, was sufficiently stolid not to be called unseemly.

The shadow waited.

With her fingers to guide her she inched past the desk, barely avoiding a collision with the chair. Now she was beginning to feel more than silly. She felt again she should call out, threaten the police, maybe throw something and run. She should, but she could not because it was only a shadow slightly darker than the others, and the hissing in her ears could indeed be the steam. Too much, they would say; first her uncle, then her lover, then the rock of the firm. Too much to handle for a woman these days.

The shadow began to melt.

She saw it and she didn't believe it: it appeared to flow into the corner, slip down toward the floor. She whirled and started for the door . . . and screamed when the door shade suddenly snapped up, racheting around its bar, the loop slapping the pane.

She screamed, and she bolted, hands out, shoulder plunging open the door and slamming it hard against the outside wall. She didn't wait for it to close; she sprinted down the alley toward the street, ready to shout at the first person she saw. Her shin clipped a trash can, and it crashed loudly behind her. She nearly fell headlong when she kicked something soft on the ground. The door clicked shut, and she closed her eyes tightly.

And she was unable to find her voice until something grabbed at her arm.

a shifting a settling an expectant satisfaction

"Miss England . . . I . . . really, I'm sorry!"

She fell back against the plate glass and looked up at the sky. An uncontrollable quivering had spread through her legs, and a pulse ticked a warning of a headache at her right temple. "Danny," she said tightly, barely moving her lips, "if you ever do that to me again, I swear I'll skin you alive."

"Honest, Miss England, I didn't mean it! You were running and I thought you were going to fall so I . . . god, Miss England, I'm really sorry."

"All right, all right," she said, just to keep him quiet. He'd begun his babbling the moment she had yelped at his touch, and he'd released her only when she tugged at her arm. When she finally lowered her gaze to meet his, not even his hangdog expression moved her to relent. "What the hell are you doing here?" she said.

He swallowed, apparently as shaken as she.

"Well?" It was a bark. She glanced quickly up and down the street, but no pedestrians were nearby, no one lounging on the corners.

"The . . ." He puffed his cheeks and blew. "It's silly, now."

"Danny!"

He pulled contritely at a forelock. "The . . . the tickets."

"The what?"

He took a step away, a step back. An elderly man carrying a brown bag soggy at its bottom hurried past them, paying them no mind as he muttered to himself.

Danny coughed into a fist. "You said . . . you said you'd let me know about a man who—"

"For god's sake, boy, does it have to be now?"

"Well . . ." He shrugged. "No, I guess not."

"I guess not," she echoed sarcastically. "If I survive this night, Danny, you'll be lucky to get them at all. God!" She put a hand to her chest, felt her heart still racing.

She did not care about the sudden hurt that narrowed his eyes, nor the way he stiffened out his small-boy stance. She left the window's support and pushed her hair back into place, smoothed her blouse, rearranged the sweater that had slipped partway off her shoulder. Did her best to ignore the whispering of the fat-boled elms that lined the curbing.

"The alley door," she said then. "Go back and see if it's locked." When he returned, trying to impress her with his speed, she ordered him inside to fetch her pocketbook, standing at the recessed doorway and staring at his shadow as it flowed ahead of him, behind him when he came back. She took the pocketbook and held it primly at her waist. "Thank you," she said stiffly.

"Miss England?"

She had already taken half a dozen steps when he called. God save me, she thought, and turned around.

"Did . . . did you mean what you said?"

"About what?" she said, impatience a rush that made her want to scream.

"The tickets."

Lord, she thought, protect me from dogs and teenage children. Her smile almost worked. "No, Danny, I didn't mean it. I was, understandably, upset."

"Wow, that's great," he said. "You . . . you don't have to be afraid of me, you know."

The smile was real this time, and he brightened and hurried to her side as she walked off. She had considered stopping at the Inn for a drink and something to eat, now had to contrive some way of shaking the boy off or she would have him on her back until she locked her door behind her. But her nerves still had not re-

covered from the fright he'd given her, were tingling in
the silence that accompanied their walking. It was
obvious he was looking for a way to say something to
her, looking for the courage to speak out. It almost
thawed her.

He touched at her arm, lightly.

She looked down at him, her lips pursed against a
smile.

His left arm swept toward the avenue, the traffic.
"All this talk about animals around and stuff," he said,
and tucked his chin close to his chest.

"Yes?"

"Well . . . you live alone."

"Yes." She drew the word out in hopes he would
know she had already taken his meaning and didn't
want to hear him voice it.

Suddenly, he was in front of her, walking backward,
his hands darting between them to emphasize his point.
"Well, see, maybe you'd like to have somebody take
care of the place for you, you know, like a private guard
or something? I wouldn't have to live in the house, I
could sleep in the shed. I don't sleep much anyway,
hardly at all. I could walk around and make sure—"

Her hand closed over a wrist and pulled him beside
her again. They were on the block midway between the
police station and the Chancellor Inn, in an island of
grey haze between two globular streetlamps buried in
the foliage. "Danny," she said, "I appreciate the offer,
really I do, but I'm sure your family would rather have
you home with them."

He looked up, down, slipped his hands into his hip
pockets. "Haven't got any."

Her mouth opened, closed; her eyes blinked slowly.

She wasn't sure if she believed him or not; the firm certainly didn't pay him enough for him to survive on his own. Other jobs, perhaps, though she didn't know when he would have the time. His expression was sullen, waiting for her to respond, and she glanced up and down the street, looking for someone she could use for an escape. But the village seemed deserted. Only the leaves overhead, scraping and rustling.

"Danny . . ." The pocketbook pressed hard against her stomach. "Danny, I've never asked you this, but where do you live?"

"Over there," he said, with a jerk of his thumb over his shoulder.

"Where, exactly, is 'over there'?"

"You know." He shrugged.

"No," she told him flatly, "I do not know. Danny, this may sound silly, but do you have anyplace to live at all?"

He frowned, a shock of black falling over his forehead. "Of course I do. You think I live with the bums on the tracks? Or in the park, maybe? I have a room, okay? One of those boarding places on Devon, all right? My folks are dead, I lie about my age, and Mr. Craig didn't care so what's the big deal, anyway?" He looked at her hard, long enough for her to turn away. "Never mind," he said. "It was just an idea, you know. I said you didn't have to be afraid of me." He walked almost stiff-legged to the corner, stopped, stared back over one hunched, sloping shoulder. "Mr. Bartelle," he said. "He isn't right for you, either."

Stunned by his audacity, Sam could only gape as he vanished behind a hedge; and by the time she recovered the presence of mind to go after him the street was empty of everything but a cat toying with a dead leaf in the center of the tarmac.

She ate at the Inn, and tasted nothing; she had a drink in the upstairs lounge, and felt nothing; she walked for nearly an hour before going home, and remembered nothing of where she had been or what she had been thinking. As if in a daze she put sweater and pocketbook away in the hall closet, walked to the kitchen and stood in front of the refrigerator. A hand reached out to grip the handle, and she shuddered at the hard chill it gave her. Vince, she thought then, had been wrong for a change: the boy had more than a simple crush on her. She had seen it in his eyes when she'd snapped at him, when she refused his offer of protection, when he'd glared at her from the corner. He was in love with her, badly, and she berated herself harshly for being so blind, wondered with a start how long she had been standing in front of the open door with an empty glass in her hand. As it was, the milk bottle hadn't nearly enough left. She took it out and placed it on the counter, went to the back door and opened it. The lid of the tin milk box was canted slightly, and she crouched to lift out the day's delivery. Hesitated, and saw Danny standing on the grass not ten feet away.

As deliberately as she could, she rose, unsure whether she was angry or afraid. "Danny," she said when she knew her voice would remain steady, "I've had quite enough of this."

He did not move.

"All right," she said, a decision made. "Maybe it would be better if you didn't come in to work tomorrow."

"You need me, Miss England."

His voice was somber, somehow deeper in the moon-light that twisted through the trees in irregular patches. It gave the air about him a silverwhite aura, blacking out his features to leave him nothing but an outline.

"Danny, I am asking you politely, and for the last time, to please leave me alone."

There were no nightsounds, no wind, the world cut away to leave her drifting.

"You need me."

He still had not moved.

"I can do just fine by myself, thank you."

The sense of a smile, of knowledge ungiven: "You need me, Miss England. I'm the only one left."

She backed into the kitchen and closed the door just short of slamming. Damn those curtains, she thought as she watched him watching the house. Her heel caught on a chair leg as she turned, and she kicked it viciously against the counter cabinets, staggering into the hallway where she hesitated in front of the telephone. Who to call first: Vince, or the police?

I'm the only one left.

The idea, the implication, that the boy had had some-thing to do with Malcolm and Reg broke gooseflesh on her arms, and she rubbed at them vigorously. But the method . . . She picked up the receiver and was told, a moment later, that Vince's line was out of order, and the line belonging to the family who lived in the other half of his duplex.

"Silly," she muttered as she headed back for the kitchen. It was just as well there was trouble; if she'd been connected she wasn't sure how she would have ex-plained it. He would have laughed, and the laugh would have put some perspective on a problem more of her creation than Danny's.

Nevertheless: *I'm the only one left*.

She glanced out the back door. Danny was gone. Then she reached for the teakettle and heard someone on the front porch.

The footfall was loud, a heel snapping against the flooring. The house picked up the sound, expanded it in the dark and gave it resonance. A second step followed, a third, a fourth. A shadow filled the translucent panes in the door; it was featureless, and flowing, like the shadow in the office. Slowly, one hand rubbing absently against her hip, she eased out of the kitchen and pressed against the staircase wall. There was less fear than there was a helpless anger: he had no right doing this to her, forcing himself on her when she had ordered him to leave. And she had no right huddling here in the dark like a child cowering against a nightmare. After all, she told herself firmly, she wasn't exactly a weakling; she could take care of herself in most instances, and especially against a thin, spindly-armed boy who wouldn't take no for an answer.

The figure on the porch moved before she did. It drifted to one side silently, and Sam hurried to the door, pressed her cheek against it and listened before feeling her way into the parlour and kneeling on the couch. The shades were up, but all she could see was the streetlamp across the street, and the tops of the shrubs beginning to give to a slow-rising wind. Frowning, she leaned closer to the window, peering through the condensation of her breath. It was an awkward position, but she could see the length of the porch, could see no one was there.

"Damn," she said.

A siren in the distance, and the Seth Thomas ticking.

Vince: *he isn't right for you, either*.

Whatever it was that had prevented her from believing shattered; either he had had a hand in the dying, or he knew what and how and was using it to scare her to him. Or had been until she denied him. And now Vince's line was down and Danny, outside, was the only one left.

The milk box tipped over; the bottles rolled across the boards. Without thinking, she rushed into the kitchen, could not bring herself to open the door but saw through a pane the Kramers' black-and-tan tom loping across the lawn after its illicit dinner. She swallowed and let a quick, relieved laugh fill the room briefly. A slow inhalation, and she decided to go after it and let it have all the milk he wanted, just for being the first friendly face she'd seen since the sun set.

The door was open and the call on her tongue when a long, thick shadow swept around the side of the shed. The tom froze when she gasped, its tail puffed and ears pricked high. It growled once, and the shadow flowed over it. Flowed over it and was gone, but not swiftly enough.

The door slammed, the lock turned after a fumbling, and as she raced for the telephone she could not help a glance over her shoulder for what the moonlight had caught, what the leaves' shadows had not hidden: the last few feet of an enormous snake's body; dark, perhaps black, and thick as a man's thigh.

You know, Malcolm had said, they eat their food alive.

You know, Vince had said, you should see all those damned teeth!

The phone was dead.

Over there, Danny had said with a jerk of his thumb.

The kitchen door slammed inward, the panes shattering and sliding across the floor. Wind followed, and moonlight, and Danny stood on the threshold . . . smiling.

"You need me," he said, and it wasn't the way he had said it before.

Sam banished thought and gave way to reflex. She whirled around and ran, leaping across the front porch to the steps, to the sidewalk, tripping into the hedge and nearly spilling into the gutter. Refusing to look around, seeing behind every post and shrub the waiting coiled form of Danny's hungry pet. It would take her, it would crush her, it would drag her away as it had the others. As she knew now it had Vincent. And if it were interrupted it would grind down to save what it could . . . and leave the rest behind.

For someone to find.

Her eyes filled with tears, and the shadows of the phone lines terrified her to whimpering.

She raced across King Street and into the hospital's waiting room, sobbing, shouting, not feeling at all the needle's jab in her arm.

David Greshton held her hand firmly while a nurse shook her clothes from the closet and lay them neatly over the footboard.

"You're sure," he said.

"I have to get my things," she told him. "I can't go like this."

"All right, but . . ."

She smiled and brought his hands to her lips—for a touch, not a kiss. For a week he had been with her, working double shifts just to give her the company, and share the dreams. They played whist and Parcheesi, listened to a radio he brought for her, and he told her that the police had searched for days without finding Danny, though the signs of his vile pet were everywhere in evidence once they knew what to look for—the droppings in the woods, the missing animals, the funnels across the wet grass and the absence of birds. He told her Uncle Leonard had died in his sleep the night of her assault, and he told her nothing of Vince had yet been discovered.

He did not have to tell her that sooner or later bones would be found, a regurgitation of what the serpent's digestion refused; sooner or later there would be something to bury.

He did not have to tell her; she knew it already.

As she dressed behind the hospital screen, he stood with his back to her and addressed the air. "It's incredible, Samantha, I still can't really believe it. He must have told one whale of a story to Craig when he was hired. No one on Devon, or in any of the other boardinghouses in town, ever heard of him. Nobody knows where he came from, or where he's gone. Actually, it's good riddance to bad rubbish, the way I see it. He was one weird kid."

No, she thought; he was frightening, he was foul.

"Do you want to wait for Angie?" he asked as he led her to the business office to effect her release.

She couldn't. She only wanted to get some fresh clothes from the house and take the next train to Hartford. From Hartford to New York. And from New York to the West Coast. In the beginning she had argued with herself that she was only running away from the tragedies that had stalked her, that she wasn't solving a thing; and leaving house and firm for so long was tantamount to economic suicide. Then Uncle Leonard's lawyer dropped by; if she chose now, she wouldn't have to work another day in her life.

Before she could change her mind, then, she had wired her friends in Los Angeles and her schoolmates in Portland, had the tickets hired and the sleeper reserved.

It would be a vacation. A release.

And if she put enough distance between herself and the Station, maybe, if she was lucky, Danny would have to find someone else to love.

With a kiss to David's cheek and a promise to write often, she left the hospital and walked as steadily as she could home. She would miss it, though; she knew she would. Before leaving she would have to call Angie to arrange for someone to take care of the yard and the shrubs, then call Tom Hancock so the police would take a turn around the property once or twice a night until she returned. Call David and thank him for saving . . . whatever was left.

She pulled her suitcases from the hall closet and lugged them up the stairs. Funny, she thought, how a house gets so musty even after a few days. As if no one lived here at all, not even me.

"No!" she declared loudly, as loudly as she could. "You're feeling sorry, Samantha, which won't solve a thing." Get on with it, kiddo, get on with it and go.

Nevertheless, she would miss it. Angie's sailor, David's fumbling, the Station itself in a Connecticut spring. She grinned as she reached the landing. Spring; how terribly symbolic. But she hoped California would live up to its billing.

And she stepped smiling into the bedroom to close out the old life.

Moving, gliding, the muted hush of ghosts slipping over thin ice clinging to black water, of sighs slipping from the lips of dead men still dying; a shifting, a settling, an expectant satisfaction.

It flowed out from beneath her bed and coiled effortlessly on the quilt.

Moving, gliding . . .

It lifted its massive head near to the ceiling and spread its black hood, its slanted red eyes fixed on hers and . . . smiling.

Nothing moved. Not the air, not the bed, not her legs, not its head.

The suitcases fell when her hands lost their feeling.

You don't have to be afraid of me.

She could see it now—silently screaming—in the way his hair was combed and flared, the odd dusk of his skin, the way he moved and talked and started when someone touched him.

She could see it, wouldn't believe it, not even when Danny's mouth opened and she could see all his teeth.

Moving . . . striking . . .

Samantha, I need you.

NOW THERE COMES
A DARKER DAY

Sunday evening in late July. When the air is drained of heat, of light, of the small cries of children and the muffled slap of heels on a sunbaked softened pavement; when furred and panting creatures crawl out from behind the latticework of porches and stretch, and yawn, and begin to prowl with no goal at all except they are tired of sleeping; when sashes are lifted and fans begin to growl; when screen doors are latched to close out the moths, and the cat, and the larger winged shadows that are drawn by the lamp; when the lingering northsound of the white ice cream truck brings to mind images of snow and skating and memories best left forgotten; when the sigh of a breeze disturbs sunweary leaves; when the darkness is a cloak to disguise the struggling failure of brittle brown grass and dusty roses.

Sunday evening in late July. When the radio at supper introduces *Yours Truly, Johnny Dollar*, and the television crackles a small round eye in the front room; when a car vibrates in silence, crawls almost apologetically into a fresh blacktop driveway, and the kids pile out, cranky and whining; when a bicycle whirrs past with a catcher's mitt on the handlebar and a bat shoved through the wire basket in the rear; when the churchbell tolls; when the park is closed.

Sunday evening in late July.

When I stand alone with a gun in my hand.

The Cock's Crow had been conceived and constructed in 1938 by an enterprising New Yorker who had slipped out of Albany (his hometown) in hopes of draining from Oxrun Station some of the money that he thought had lain fallow during the years of the Depression. Most admitted it wasn't a half-bad idea. If you did not eat at the Chancellor Inn or the Centre Street Luncheonette, and you didn't have the means or the time or the energy to make the drive north into Harley, you were usually stuck in your Formica kitchen staring at leftovers. It seemed a natural and probably might have been, under more reliable, less greedy supervision. But Eban Thonger had no idea what the Station was like save what he heard through gossip; no idea at all. So a perfect mile from the village he built a long, low building of log cabin design that faced Mainland Road from behind a graveled parking lot and beneath a sign that, when lighted, could be seen from the hill in the middle of the park. Then he added glaring lights inside, small tables, the largest jukebox in the state, waitresses who didn't mind showing the backs of their knees when they delivered an order at the next table, and a bar that carried more beers and cheap liquors than any four dives in Hartford.

He was an obsequious, pencil-mustached man and his lack of understanding sent him bewildered into bankruptcy less than a year later.

The following summer Susan and Todd Kranepool picked up the pieces and renamed it after themselves. They threw out the jukebox, the waitresses, the beer and the liquor, clapped aluminum across the front and called it a diner instead of a roadhouse. They were a charming if somewhat coarse couple from Hartford, and they managed to reach the spring of 1941 before the bank moved in and they moved out.

In 1942 a local man, Wallace Inness, picked it up at sheriff's auction and somehow managed to turn it into a bordello that lasted a full six months before a church warden blew the whistle.

In 1943 it nearly burned down when a rails rider caught himself on fire while smoking a cigar and drinking his daily sterno ration.

Then it sat for two years, black and ugly and falling prey to the rain before I gave up my old job and bought it myself. It was, in part, a celebration: the end of one life, the beginning of another. The first thing I did was strip off that hideous aluminum. Then I restored its old name and proceeded to dim the lights and widen the tables; I added a mahogany bar ten feet long in a leather-and-brass-rimmed crescent, had four waitresses working in two shifts each day (except for a trio on Saturday nights), and found a cook in Bangor who didn't much care for whites but couldn't bring himself to stay away from the salary I paid him and the new equipment I let him pick out. The walls were paneled with a shimmering black oak, the pegged floors sanded and polished, and the fresh blacktop over the parking lot was swept clean every morning.

It was bonecracking, absolutely masochistic work restoring that place, and it gave me calluses where I never believed they could crop up on a human being. But it also gave me a chance to do something with my hands that had no connection at all with writing out speeding tickets, holding a gun on a nervous, two-bit burglar or climbing a tangled willow to fetch Mrs. Bartlett's fat-butt tom who didn't have the brains to remember he was scared to death of heights.

And in spite of all the complaining I did, all the swearing, all the imprecations against gods determined to prevent me from resting at last, I loved it. I had built myself a small cottage back in the trees behind the road-house, and when I woke up in the morning I could look out my kitchen window and see the Cock's Crow. Sitting there. Sleeping, waiting, maybe seeing Righteous O'Hara there on the back stoop with his first cigar of the day, enjoying the air. His white cap and apron would already be on, and smoke from the warming ovens would be wafting from the chimney. If I were lucky, he'd be in a good mood and I wouldn't have to make my own breakfast.

And as I'd hoped—knowing I would fail otherwise, just like the others—the roadhouse became a place where folks who didn't have the price of a couple of hours in the Chancellor Inn could come and enjoy them-selves—with twenty-four different kinds of sandwiches (most of them hot), lots of conversation, a drink or two; they could, most importantly, relax and have a fine time without someone over in the corner glaring as if they were shouting in a library. Those who didn't like it—and there were a few, quite a few—never came back; those who did came often, became regulars, and it was no time at all before I could haul myself out of bed most days and not once miss getting into a uni-form.

"I don't care," said Paul Hollander late one Friday afternoon when I mentioned this feeling to him. "You stand back there in your shirtsleeves, or you sit by the register, your eyes watching every damn thing that moves, you still look like a cop.''

"I really appreciate that, Paul."

"Don't mention it," he said. "Just keep those thoughts to yourself from now on, if you don't mind." He grinned, shifting jowls and wattles far too numerous for a man his age. "Remember, we're the ones who're supposed to be telling you our troubles, not the other way around.''

"Troubles I don't have at the moment, thank you," I told him. "And I'm not a bartender, damnit. I'm just filling in—''

We laughed, as we always did every Friday afternoon. It was ritual; sometimes tedious, but nonetheless a comfort. He, and most of the other high school and grade school teachers, made it a point to stop by once classes were over and their paychecks cashed. Luckily, the bar had not been intended to be the Crow's drawing card, because few of them wanted to start blurring their weekends so early, especially now, as summer sessions drew to a close and their vacations loomed with munificent temptations. As a matter of fact, I never had serious problems with drunks, even on Saturdays. There was something about the place, about the people who liked it and claimed it for their own, that prohibited inhibitions from ranging too far from home.

Sandy Fielder came in just about then, puffing as though he'd run all the way from the village, shucking his coat onto the rack by the front door, stopping once at a table to listen to Harry Jackson complain about the barkeep's son's grades in junior English. Sandy did what he always did: he promised to switch the boy (who was a foot taller and forty pounds heavier), and offered the teacher a drink on the house. I didn't mind all that much. Sandy practically lived here, and one glass of bourbon wasn't going to break me.

"Sorry, Tom," he said as he slid into place. The hair that gave him his name was cropped in a marine's cut, his shoulders as broad, his paunch poised to engulf his belt.

"No sweat. How's Marie?"

He shrugged. His wife had been stricken with polio nine years before, and though the doctors had told her she could walk if she tried—with an aid, of course—she apparently had grown to enjoy the special bed in her room, and the service it brought her . . . and the guilt it gave her husband whenever he left her.

We didn't have much time to talk after that. The dinner hour arrived, and Righteous bellowed for my help back at the stoves. I worked with him gladly, saying nothing, watching the concentration on his walnut-dark face until the flow eased. Then I grabbed myself a hamburger and went into my small office where I ate, changed my shirt, washed my face and returned to the front to see who was left for the passing of the night.

And was stopped by the almost perfect silence that filled the room.

I looked to Sandy. He tilted his head to the left-hand front corner.

It was nearly eight o'clock by then, and Grace (who should have been my partner for all the work she did when she didn't have to) had dimmed the lamps ensconced in their pine wall brackets, drawn the gold-edged russet curtains and lighted the candles on each of the tables. The waitresses' smiles were more genuine now that the hassles were done, and they stopped for conversations without straining people's patience. It was, as someone once told me, more a club atmosphere than a roadhouse; and like a club there were characters.

One of them was Rexall Joseph Stephenson.

Not really a character, I suppose and if I have to be honest. A mainstay, rather, and a friend. And, like most of my friends, just a little bit lonely. He was well over six feet tall, heavyset, a man who moved slowly with a slight swaying shuffle, almost as though he were permanently aboard ship. His hair was deep black, his full beard thick and lumberjack wild, and he sat in that corner every Friday night daring folks to catch him with a poetry line. He loved verse, any and all kinds from Donne to doggerel, and as long as I'd known him he'd never once had to pay the check for his own meals or drink. He was also about the most morose man I ever met. If it wasn't the North Koreans who were currently leading us into Armageddon, it was the inflation that ate the inheritance his mother had left him. He wept when the American League lost the All-Star game, when Ohio State took the Rose Bowl, when I installed air conditioning to keep the customers from fainting on nights like this. Nothing pleased Rex. Nothing ever would.

And tonight he was sitting at his table with the biggest grin a man could muster.

I took a seat opposite him, my back to the room, and folded my arms on the table. Though I was nearly as tall (not nearly as brawny), I felt like a child before a slightly plastered uncle.

Ritual, then; always the ritual before the evening began. Put a nickel in the slot and wait for the music. The music, for me, however, was a couple of hundred years old.

" 'Its passion will rock thee,' " I said, in a monotone that destroyed the poem I was quoting, " 'as the storms rock the ravens of high.' "

Rex sighed loudly and shook his head at my shame. "Shelley," he told me, just this side of disgust. "*The Flight of Love*. Thomas, you are going to have to do better than that."

"I've been sick," I said, unsuccessfully trying to hide a smile. And I didn't dare tell him that it took me nearly a week to dig that one up; he would have pitied me, at the top of his marvelous voice, for the rest of the night.

"Do you have another?" Lord, it was like watching the proverbial cat at a veritable feast of canaries. The man just would not stop grinning.

Before I could answer, though, Harry Jackson squirmed between tables and stood beside me. Harry was Rex's potential nemesis, more likely (except to Harry) Rex's Abbott to Harry's determined and ill-fated Costello.

"Fire away," Rex told him, with a soft wink to me.

Harry pulled himself up confidently, though not confidently enough to lift his voice above a whisper. " 'This must be done with haste, for night's swift dragons cut the clouds full fast.' And by god, I didn't misquote it this time." He waited. "So?"

Rex stared at him, at me, looked up to the ceiling in the most blatant of feigned concentrations I have ever seen outside the dual cogitations of Harpo and Chico Marx. It was a terrible sight, and without looking I could see Harry beginning to wilt.

"The trouble is, you see," Rex said, "I don't really care for Shakespeare all that much."

Harry groaned.

"And I especially don't like that little bastard, Robin Goodfellow. They call him Puck, but I've another word for that . . . and I suspect, strongly suspect, that the original folio that contains the play holds the same word I'm thinking of now." He leaned forward, then, his forearms on the table, looking at Harry earnestly, as though the two of them were about to decide the fate of Asia. "I mean, really, Harry, don't you think he's a bit much? All the other faeries, sprites, whatever you want to call them, they're sweet, they're harmless, their pranks aren't dangerous at all. Puck, on the other hand, is a first class, A-number one—"

"Rex," Harry interrupted, "would you mind finishing me off so I can go back to my table?"

Rex, clearly, was disappointed. He definitely wanted to carry on, and Jackson was taking away much of his fun. "Damn. All right. *A Midsummer Night's Dream*, okay? The second act . . . no, the third act, the second scene. Little bastard."

Harry nodded once, sharply, and left. Then Rex turned to me and the grin was back. "You have a pitcher in the bullpen, I assume?"

"Just one," I said.

"Well?"

"You'll be gentle?"

"Thomas," he warned. The ritual, apparently, was interfering with whatever news he had that was waiting too long for the telling he wanted.

"Okay, okay. 'Now is come a darker day, and thou soon must be his prey.' Wise guy."

"Lord," he said, "you really are depressed to-night. Shelley, again. *Notes Written in the Euganean Hills, North Italy*. Or words to that effect. Are you all right?"

"I'm fine," I said. "You, however, never cease to amaze me."

"Want to bet? How about this: Thomas Gaines Hancock, I am in love."

"Yes?" I didn't bat an eyelash, a feat that disconcerted him.

"You doubt me, right?" he said. His Princeton tie was straight, his hair combed, his black-rimmed glasses set square in their place. "Well, I don't care, you hear me? I, sir, am in love. Period."

This time my smile was strained. I felt uneasy because I didn't know, after all these years of predictability, how to handle this change, this alteration of ritual. But as the background conversations renewed themselves and the evening began in earnest, I decided to let him have that benefit of those doubts. And he was right: doubts I had. Another thing Rex did with persistent regularity was fall in love. Though I had to admit that he'd never grinned before. Usually it was a solemn proclamation, accompanied by a deep grumbling in his chest as though a Gregorian chant were struggling to break free. He would then index her qualities, admit to her faults and once even talked himself out of it before he had shut up.

But by god, the man had never grinned before.

"Her name," he said, "is Elizabeth Corey."

I tried to place her, to put a face to the name. The Station isn't so small that you know everyone who lives here, but names are hard to forget, especially when learning them and remembering had once been part of my job. But Elizabeth Corey did not strike the faintest of echoes.

"You don't know her," he told me, sensing my loss as if it were indeed my loss. He leaned back and pulled his beer glass toward him, studied the foam head thoughtfully, then looked down at me over the tops of his lenses. "Funny," he said. "It's funny. It's like one of those movies, you know? You say to yourself that something like that can never happen, not in a million years, and the next thing you know you've been written into the script. Funny."

"What?" I said quietly. "What's funny about it, Rex?"

"Well, I was coming home from a meeting late last Tuesday, and I saw her—Elizabeth—coming out of the park. There was a little girl with her. The girl was crying and holding her arm, so, being the naturally gallant gentleman, I offered them my services. The lady accepted and, as it turned out, the wound was little more than a nasty scrape easily cleaned and bound with my handkerchief. We walked, then, the three of us, and before I can say nay there was a late dinner at the Inn—sorry, Thomas, but I was frankly out to impress; damn, sorry again—and when the little girl told me they were out looking for a boardinghouse, I happened to let it drop that I had occasion to rent out a room now and then, for special people." He smiled apologetically, knowing I hadn't realized his finances were so tight. "Since Mother died, it isn't easy keeping such a large house, even with the money she left me."

I waved away the explanation; coming as it had from a friend of long standing, it wasn't at all necessary.

"Anyway, I assured her of my intentions, as they used to put it, and the invitation was accepted. Ah, Thomas, you have no idea. You have no idea at all!"

I did, but I wasn't about to say anything and break his bubble, and I couldn't have done it even if I'd wanted. At that moment he straightened suddenly, brightened, and when I turned around there were no introductions needed.

Elizabeth Corey was not particularly stunning, nor ethereal, nor even what the English call handsome. Nevertheless, there was something about her, the way she moved from the door to the table, the way her dress fell in velveteen folds to the tops of her shoes, the way her hair took fire and sun to her shoulders . . . It was the way of her, and for a moment I had never felt more lonely in my life.

And it was the way, too, of the child who walked with her. A darker version of the same woman, petticoats and saddle shoes, white ribbons in her hair. I guessed her about ten, and certainly no more, probably less. And I might have been more polite, I suppose, had I not seen the way her mother held her hand—so tightly the child's fingers were nearly turning red. The girl didn't seem to mind, however, the shyness of her glance perfectly matching a nosegay of four violets pinned to her white collar.

I rose, nodded to the woman, smiled at the child and backed off to leave them. She had said nothing to me, but I didn't have to hear her. The voice would be quiet, perhaps a Virginia-born lilt, and the child would be the same, only crystal and high. I didn't have to hear her, and it was just as well I didn't; there's not much an ex-cop and roadhouse proprietor can say to someone like that.

Hollander met me at the bar when I took my place beside the register. The seats atop their black swivels were higher-backed than usual, comfortably padded, with armrests that more rightly belonged to club chairs and lounges. I settled in, Sandy raised an eyebrow at me and I shrugged; Grace, all blonde and willows and green-eyed Irish, sat on my left with an exaggerated sigh.

"Charming," she whispered, her lips so close to my ear I could feel her breath. The world was of the opinion we would marry someday.

"Jealous," I said.

Hollander laughed, a little too loudly and I looked to him quickly. Though he was turned toward me and fingering his bow tie, he was watching the corner intently. The look was there; he was already thinking of how to be a rival.

"You know her?" I asked.

"No," he said. It sounded as if he were choking. "Lovely, isn't she?"

"I've seen better," Grace said, and slid out of her seat. Her hand lingered on my forearm and I patted it absently.

"No," Hollander told her as she made her way to a side table. "No, no better, Thomas."

"Well, maybe she is lovely," I said, "but did you catch the way she was holding that kid's hand? Any tighter and it would have fallen off."

Hollander glared at me, startling me so much I leaned back and grabbed for the bar's leather padding. "You know what your problem is, Tom? Do you ever think about your problem? You spend too much time in here, that's what. You still think like a cop. And you don't pay any attention to what's going on outside there. Did it ever occur to you that perhaps that litle girl did something terribly wrong outside and was being punished? Or perhaps she and her mother had an argument of some kind?''

It hadn't occurred to me, but neither did I think it likely. Either that, or Elizabeth Corey was the best actress in the world . . . and the child a close second.

"Listen, Paul," I said, ready to make amends for whatever it was I'd done wrong, "I just happen to have here a new deck of cards. Never before touched by human hands. What do you say we deal our Friday hand and see—"

"No," Paul said. He dropped a bill on my hand and walked away, angling toward Stephenson and the company he was drawing. I looked to Sandy for a reaction, and some support, but he too was captured by the web spinning over there; and as I glanced around the room I noticed that no one else—or rather, none that I could see—seemed to be as taken by the Coreys as were me and my friends.

Paul reached the table, turned around and scowled, turned back and sat when Rex pulled out a chair. I suppose I should have gotten angry, or at least showed some emotion, but I couldn't. I had done too much of that patrolling the Station's streets, gotten too involved in too many people's problems, people whose lives then drifted away from me once business was done and I was a uniform again. So I had taught myself to swallow it, crush it, until I was sure I wouldn't be drowned again . . . and left to drift. Maudlin, self-pitying—I know all that, but it had served me quite well thus far, and I saw no reason to change now. No reason, that is, except perhaps Grace.

Eliabeth Corey.

That feeling of loneliness dissipated slowly, but what was left was an uneasiness I told myself was nerves—a worrying for Rex, and maybe just a bit of wistful, wishful thinking.

By the end of the evening Grace had had enough of Rex's bellowings for champagne, and enough of the small party swirling over there in the corner. She rested next to me, pulling at the dark ribbon that held her hair from her face. We said nothing to each other, only bantered with Sandy, who was preparing to close down. Customers left, bills were paid and the party continued. I started for it once to give it an end, but Grace touched me on the elbow and slowly shook her head. In a way she was right: the sight of Rex laughing like that, hearing his voice raised in something other than melodramatic fury, was well worth hanging on to for as long as we could. So midnight passed, and one, and finally there were only the three of them, and the three of us. And Rex at last bowed low at the waist, nearly struck his nose on the table, and Elizabeth and the child took him away.

Not once did they glance in our direction.

Not once had I heard the woman speak, or the child giggle or laugh.

"Enough, by god," Sandy said. He rolled his apron ceremoniously and tucked it under his arm like a swagger stick. Nodded. Departed. Grace slipped into a light sweater and kissed me on the cheek.

"Don't take it so hard," she said, ruffling my hair because she knew how I hated it. "Friends do get married now and then, you know."

Righteous was the last to leave. He said nothing to

me, only grumbled to himself, switched off the kitchen lights and used the rear exit.

Quiet; a deafening sound once filled with chatter, and I almost switched on the radio to keep me company. Instead, I wasted some time straightening a tablecloth here, a lampshade there, tying back the curtains and turning off the outside lights. Then I stared out at the road, at the occasional truck that muttered by, the once-in-a-while automobile that slowed until it realized the Cock's Crow was closed.

The air conditioning was off, and perspiration began gathering down my spine. I stepped outside to breathe, and thought of what Grace had said. Marriage, however, hadn't entered my mind, but I guess somewhere back there I knew it was inevitable. Rex was too much the poseur to escape such a challenging role.

With hands in my pockets, then, I strolled around the corner of the building, thinking that I was probably just as ridiculous a figure as my friend. I kicked at a pebble, a stone . . . and stopped, lifting my head as if someone had called me. Paul can deride my former profession all he wants, but something halted me then. Yet, when I turned around suddenly and stared at the wall of woodland on the other side of the road, there was nothing. No sound, no movement, not a hint of anything wrong.

I looked back at the cottage, at the porch light, at my bedroom window above.

I looked at the Cock's Crow.

And without knowing why—and hating myself for it—I wished aloud Grace had stayed with me, and Elizabeth Corey was dead.

A week passed that was unusual only in that it was

virtually uneventful. I did not see either Rex or Paul again, nor did I see the woman and her child those times when I was in town to do some shopping. I was tempted to call, but talked myself out of it each time with the admonition that Rex was a big boy now, that I was only feeling depressed last Friday and thus open to all sorts of unpleasant sensations, and if I didn't mind my own business I would probably be slugged.

Friday night, however, Rex didn't show for his corner display.

And on Saturday morning a sacrosanction was violated: I had two phone calls well before noon. Normally, I did not bother to even look at the receiver since all my friends knew better than to ruin my sleeping late. It was a luxury I permitted myself because, in spite of the roadhouse's success, I was not about to let it guide me into an early grave. It was my place to enjoy, not to have it run me; and to enjoy it I opened late on Saturdays; four o'clock, in fact. That gave me enough time to test my pillow for defects, to take rides in my Hudson or read in the library or, as I'd planned for today, walk over to the park and listen to the concert.

Either a salesman or an emergency, I decided, rubbing the sleep from my eyes and scowling at the floor. I sat on the edge of the bed and yawned. The phone continued to ring. No salesman was that persistent, I thought miserably.

It was Paul; and though I could detect no panic or hysteria in his voice, there was a tone there I could not identify, one that made him sound distant, sound odd.

"Hey, about last Friday night," he said, "I . . . Well, my nephew—you may know him, Frank Blaine— he was called up on Wednesday. I'm sure he's going to be sent over, you see, and he's really all the family I have left. I . . . I suppose I was—"

"Don't worry about it, Paul." Still groggy, I sucked at my teeth to get rid of the cotton growing there.

There was a pause, then, that set me wondering.

"Ah . . . Tom?"

"Still here, though you obviously haven't looked at your clock in the last hour or so."

"Sorry."

"Don't mention it." I grinned at the opposite wall. Paul could be made to feel guilty about the sun rising or Truman's language.

"Say, you remember that woman Rex is going to marry? Elizabeth, I think her name is."

I stuck my tongue out at the mouthpiece, kept my voice flat. "I remember her. What's the matter?"

"I don't think she wants to marry him."

Finally I was awake, and whatever charity I'd been feeling had been replaced by sullen curiosity. "What? What makes you say a thing like that?"

His voice lowered even more, and I found myself leaning forward as though he were in the same room and whispering behind a hand. "Because I know, that's how I know."

"And that doesn't make a damned bit of sense, Paul. Come on, what gives?"

"Tom, I really don't know what to say. That is, I do know, but I don't know how it's going to sound, we being friends together and all. It's . . . I just don't know. How to say it, that is."

I warned him with a growl that may have been his name.

"All right, all right! I don't think so . . . I don't

think so, Tom, because she's here, with me, now.''

I looked up at the wall over my chest of drawers, at the framed picture of my folks in front of their Colorado home, at the aerial photograph of Manhattan I had cut from an old *Look* because of the lights that reminded me too much of stars. ''What do you mean,'' I said as slowly as I could, ''she's there now.''

''Just what I said,'' he told me, confidence somewhat returned. ''When I got up—you know I'm an early riser, matter of habit—when I got up and went out for the paper she was standing on the porch with the kid. And Tom . . . she has a black eye.''

''Who's got a black eye?''

''Elizabeth.''

I rubbed a hand hard over my face, through my hair, over my thighs until they reddened. ''How?''

''She says Rex gave it to her.''

Immediately, I recognized what was wrong with the teacher's voice: there was a suppressed rage there, a subterranean boiling looking for the crack that would free it in explosion. In twelve years of knowing him, I'd never heard it before.

''That's not right,'' I said, as calmly as I could. ''Damnit, you know him, Paul, you know him as well as I do. He wouldn't hurt a fly, he even hates the zoo. And you can't blame it on drinking: he falls asleep when he gets drunk, for god's sake. Strike a woman? Elizabeth? Forget it. That's wrong. It's not true.''

''Elizabeth doesn't lie.''

''What does the kid say?''

''Nothing. She's sitting by her mother now, just holding her hand and . . . I . . . oh my god, Tom, what am I going to do?''

"Nothing," I said quickly to the panic in the question. I swallowed, waited, listened to him breathe. "Fix the eye best you can, give them something to eat. Then, when you've calmed down, give Rex a call and find out the truth. Good god, Paul, I'm not your father, you know."

The rage was back, its direction altered. "You really are a cold fish, aren't you, Tom," he said quietly, and rang off before I could reply.

There was no sense in trying to sleep again, so I pushed myself from the bed, disgruntled and grumbling, and took a dissatisfying shower. The day's heat was already crawling into the shadows, the dim light made by the drawn curtains and shades, and I had almost written off my friend's queer behavior to heatstroke or worse when the telephone rang again. I hoped it was Rex. I had tried his place twice before heading for the bathroom, and there'd been no answer. I wasn't surprised; knowing him, he was probably garbed in sackcloth and out looking for Miss Corey, lumbering through the street like a lost bear in search of honey.

I was right.

"Thomas, I—"

"Where the hell have you been?" I snapped. "I've been trying to get you all morning."

He did not answer immediately, and I could bring to mind no image of him standing in the hallway of that white elephant he'd inherited. And that was curious; usually, I could tell from his tone what posture he had taken. Now, however, there was only a moment's silence and an odd hissing on the line—or, rather, in the background, sounding through his home.

"Rex?"

"Thomas, she's gone."

"Yes, I know. Paul just called me in a hell of a panic. She's gone over there, was there when he got up this morning." I waited. "Rex, what happened?"

"She's gone, Thomas."

"I know, Rex. Just tell me what happened, all right? Paul says she has a black eye. She claims you gave it to her."

"I want her back, Thomas. I need her."

I took a deep breath and held it, released it slowly. Patience was what I needed now. He wasn't whining or threatening; it was more than anything, supplication. And it frightened me.

"Listen," I said, "we'll take care of it, Rex, don't worry. But first I have to know if you really—"

"Thomas, what's it doing over there?"

Over here? It was just over two miles from the roadhouse to Stephenson's home; whatever it was doing here it was doing over there. "It's baking, Rex, the same as it's been for the last week. I would fry an egg on the parking lot, but Righteous would quit because I was moving in on his territory."

"No," he said.

"I know that," I said, unable to conceal a small swell of disgust. "I was just kidding, for god's sake."

I blinked, but pulled aside the shade just in case. The sun was white, the colors bleached. As far as I could tell, the nearest clouds were in Canada. "No," I said. "Rex, what's going on?"

"It's raining," he insisted. "There's thunder, the gutters are stopped up, I can smell ozone from the lightning."

"Rex, listen to me, friend—there is no rain. There is no thunder. It's hot out there."

I heard him catch his breath, the background hissing muffled as if he'd placed the receiver against his chest. Then a scratching, a labored sound. A scuffling as though he were walking around the foyer to the limit of the phone's cord. I said nothing because he obviously wasn't listening—either to me or to himself; I would have to wait until he calmed; so I could get through to him without shouting.

"Thomas?"

He sounded as though he were being strangled. "Still here, Rex, still here."

"My god," he whispered through a clearing of his throat. "My god, Thomas, I didn't mean it."

"If you're talking about what I think you're talking about, it was a lousy joke, Rex."

"Jesus, I didn't mean it!"

I wanted to climb through the phone, then, and grab hold of his neck. "Rex, for crying out loud, calm down, damnit! You weren't the first man in the world to hit a woman, you know. And you sure won't be the last. For god's sake—"

"But I didn't, Thomas! You know me better than that. I never touched that . . . woman. It was the child, don't you see? She was always there, whenever I turned around she was there, with her mother. Confound it, I love Elizabeth, Thomas. I wouldn't hurt her for the world. I've never met anyone like her, not in all these years. But that child, Thomas. She was always there. Then she gave me a—"

He yelled suddenly, more like a shriek. There was an electrical *pop!* on the line that forced the receiver away

from my ear, and before I could recover the connection
had been broken. I shouted Rex's name futilely several
times, then called the operator and waited for a minute
that seemed more like an hour before she returned to tell
me the telephone was out of order. I didn't waste any
time arguing with her; I slammed the receiver into its
cradle, was dressed and in my car in less than five
minutes, wincing at the scorching seats, hissing when I
tried to grab the steering wheel and still maneuver
without crashing. Then I raced to the Stephenson home,
a large, gable-encumbered Georgian on the north side of
Chancellor Avenue, on the far side of the park. Up the
drive through a tunnel of heat-laden elms, out of the car
almost before it stopped.

My shirt was drenched with perspiration, my hair
plastered to my forehead and temples and feeling as
though I'd been doused with slime. I had to lean against
the fender for a moment or two just to catch a breath of
air not quite fresh, though it was not as stifling as it had
been in the car.

The heat, I thought; mad dogs and Englishmen and
the Queen must be nuts.

I mopped my face with a forearm and moved on,
suddenly reluctant.

The front door was ajar (though not wide enough for
a man to pass through), and I pushed at it with one
finger, thinking absolutely unreasonably that there was
someone hiding behind it, ready to leap out at
me—though to shout *boo!* or plunge a dagger I could
not have said. The hinges creaked, as if balking at
permitting the sun access to the grey slate foyer and the
fan-shaped staircase beyond. I stepped over the threshold (holding my breath until I wasn't stabbed) and

called out. There was no answer, not even an echo. I coughed loudly, then called again . . . and still there was nothing.

A breeze followed me in, cat-soft and sneaking, chilling the back of my neck and forcing me silently across the slate to the butler's table set against the staircase wall. On it was the telephone, and I stared at it stupidly, reached out one finger and touched at it; it was warm, and no warmer than it should have been for the furnace smoldering inside. Despite the breeze the air was unmoving, tasting stale, as if none of the windows on any of the floors had been open for a month. I poked at the phone again, then stepped back and noticed with a puzzled frown that I had left a footprint in large swirls of pale dust that reached out from the table's legs. The breeze gusted, the dust was gone, and lying hard against the baseboard was a small, blackened piece of cardboard. I dropped slowly into a crouch to get a better look, and when I reached out to pick it up, I was surprised to see that it was a flower. It was, in fact, a violet that looked as if it had been held deliberately over an open flame until it had writhed into a sickening spiral. I thought instantly of the nosegay on the child's dress, dropped the rest of the way to my knees to search for signs of further scorching.

And as soon as I decided there was none, I rose again and took out a handkerchief to blot at my face while I made my way through all the first-floor rooms.

I had not been in Stephenson's house a good many times, as many people have supposed because of our closeness, but as far as I could tell everything was as it should have been. Except Rex was not here.

Upstairs it was the same.

By the time I returned outside I was swallowing hard for air, and even the oven that called itself the outdoors was preferable to what I had left behind. My legs were somewhat wobbly from all that climbing and ducking, so I dropped onto the low stoop and let my hands sag over my knees. I could not move for several minutes; my eyes burned, my throat scratched, and I must have gone through every trick in the book to keep myself from passing out before I noticed, between slow blinks, the puddles drying out on the walk. I leaned to my left and pressed a palm against the ground: the grass was brown and dry, but the earth beneath was waterdark and spongy. I stood and backed away toward my car; I could see diamond droplets on a few of the windows, the stone beneath the sills streaked wetly and fading. It was the same all around the house, and when I looked in one of the rain barrels, there was fresh water glinting in the bottom.

I couldn't help checking a hose I found coiled beneath a spigot; the dirt at the nozzle was caked hard and old.

I did not attempt to construct an explanation. Not yet. I was still reacting to Rex's frantic call, to the deserted silence of the house and grounds, and to try to make more of damp earth than that it constituted an invitation to a prenoon bout of drinking. Let the thinking come later, I told myself as I headed quickly back to the car; right now I had to get away from the dead-eyed windows that reflected things I just as soon didn't want to see.

Ten minutes later I found a place to park, in front of the venerable grade school on High Street. I walked to the corner slowly, glanced blindly up and down Centre Street, then ducked into the luncheonette, where I had a long, tasteless meal. Lots of coffee. A few hesitant smiles from the waitress, who, I knew, wanted to razz me about eating here instead of my own place. When I was done, forgetting immediately what had been placed before me, I headed back past my car and through the iron-spear gates that led into the park.

I sighed. Though Oxrun was exceptional, even it needed a place where one could hide if needed, could imagine there was nothing in the world but children playing and lovers courting. Could imagine that a heavy rainstorm in one place didn't necessarily mean it had to be the same in another.

I meandered along the blacktop paths that branched out from the entrance, oases of greylight slanting through the gaps of hickory, ash, red maple and oak. I shivered in response to the sudden drop in temperature, had to shade my eyes to look beyond the boles and thick shrubbery to the playing fields beyond. There I could see singles, couples and families already gathering for the biweekly band concert, picnic baskets and sun umbrellas in hand, the places where the slow-shifting light would eventually flee already staked out by those willing to take the heat now for a promise of later relief. There was only one baseball game in progress, and it was desultory, a winding through the motions because Saturday afternoon wouldn't be a true Saturday afternoon without it. The moment the first note was struck in the huge gazebo, however, everything would stop, duty done, permission given to lie down and doze.

I moved on, however, in no need of company, rounding the kiosks and small pavilions that sold snacks to the youngsters who had conned their parents, newspapers for those who had conned themselves. The ground rose gently and I followed it upward, heading for the summit of the low hill that centered the park. Just before I reached it, I cut through the underbrush to the grassy slope on the other side, using the twisted, drooping limbs of an ancient weeping elm as a screen for shade while I perched on my favorite root and gazed down. At the gazebo where the band in its crimson was already setting up, at the ballfields lifting faint red dust into the useless breeze, at the sweep of trees on the left that surrounded the pond. Generally, that spring-fed L-shaped body of water was too cold for swimming, but now I could hear gusts of laughter, of shrieks, the *crack* of bat-and-ball, the admonition of a mother to a child playing with a stray dog; the wind was right, and I would be able to hear the music without leaving the shade.

It wasn't that I disliked people or their company; I just didn't feel like doing any talking just yet. I wasn't about to go to the police; young Abe Stockton, or one of the other patrolmen, would only take me back to the house to show me what I'd missed, the perfectly reasonable explanation for the desertion, and the rain. Which is why I also hadn't called Paul Hollander, either. I was, frankly, feeling a little bit stupid, working myself into a hot-weather lather over something I knew had the most simple of answers; and what I didn't need then was someone pointing it out before I'd discovered it myself. Pride, I suppose. And I knew if I had any brains I'd call Hollander now and get it over with before the rest of my day was ruined with inaction.

And I had just about decided to get up and go when the band began playing, having obviously come to the conclusion there was no better way to pass a July afternoon than with Gershwin. Nobody, not even my sheepish stupidity, could move me with an enticement like that, a web of muted brass that settled over you like a shawl of indolent gossamer, that magnified the sounds of the swimming and the playing; it ignored the clock, it ignored the sun, and anyone who moved a muscle for more than the banishment of a pesky fly was more crazy than I, worrying about Rex.

I dozed, feeling the music and not caring about the grin I felt on my face.

I daydreamed—about the Cock's Crow, about Grace, about Grace and me, about the livin' that was easy for Grace and me . . . about Rex telling me frantically he didn't mean it. Didn't mean it. The hissing, the crackling, and suddenly the dead line.

I opened my eyes and almost strangled on a choked, startled cry.

Elizabeth Corey was standing in front of me, the girl-child clinging to her pleated white skirt and sucking her thumb.

Too embarrassed by my reaction to speak, I sat up quickly and motioned them to sit by me if they wished. The girl sat between us, knees drawn up and hands gripping them loosely. Elizabeth stretched out her legs and folded her hands in her lap. Though I kept glancing over the little one to her, there was no response at all, nothing but a calm, almost blank gazing down the slope to the band.

But she was beautiful, and I didn't know why I hadn't seen it that clearly the first night. Haloed with leaves, touched by the sun, framed by a background of white birch, she seemed a bas-relief from some unknown Monet, a ghost of Renoir, specks and dots and whispers of pastels that congealed into something that could only be shattered if disturbed.

It grew hotter, but I did not move to wipe the perspiration from my arms, my chin, the sides of my neck. As Gershwin wove, I nodded while my hands fluttered to accompany the dream.

There was no sound but the music.

Finally, when the band lowered its instruments for a refreshment break and the small crowd stirred as if newly awakened, I turned to Elizabeth and asked her if she knew why Rex hadn't been home earlier this afternoon. I'd meant to ask the reason for their spat, but the words had somehow rearranged themselves when I noticed her eye—clear, unblemished, not a cell damaged or a mote of discoloration visible. Paul strikes again, I thought somewhat sourly, and Rex is vindicated, at least of abuse.

She turned to me and lifted her shoulders in a faint shrug.

"Paul called me, you know," I said. I forced a laugh. "I hope he doesn't go storming over there and demand a duel or something. He's like that, you see. Rex may be the poet, but Hollander is the chevalier."

The quiver on her lips may have been a smile.

"I know," I said, absently brushing at the little girl's sunwarm hair. "That doesn't sound like a cop, does it—or rather, a guy who used to be a cop. But as you've already no doubt noticed, this place isn't your run-of-the-mill community, either. I have a friend I used to work with when he first came on the force, Abe

Stockton. I think he's the only member of the force who hasn't gone to college.'' I laughed again and shook my head. "Like the last election. I could give you five dollars for every man you meet who voted for Truman, and I'd still have enough left over to buy a Cadillac. Crazy." I waited. "Crazy." Waited again. "Is . . . that is, are you staying with Paul—never mind, never mind, it's none of my business. I just wish I knew where Rex had gone. He tends to the histrionic now and then.''

I couldn't help it. I knew how I sounded, and I just couldn't help it.

I tried to be tactful. "Look, I hope what cropped up between you two isn't going to ruin the engagement." A glance at her hand; there was no ring, or signs one had been there. "I mean, Paul was a little hysterical when he called me this morning, to tell the truth, and I'd think . . . well, if you don't mind me saying so, you really don't look all that broken up about it. Most women I know would be after the man with a cleaver, or crying their eyes out, you know what I mean? Of course, Rex has a habit of seeing things that aren't there, and maybe you two weren't—"

Suddenly, the little girl jumped to her feet just as the band started the second half of its program. She grinned down at me, took a feigned swipe at my chin and raced into the trees behind us. Elizabeth looked over her shoulder, a hand nervously to her lips.

"It's all right," I said. "I'll get her back." I wanted to add a reassuring pat to her arm, her back, but I didn't. Instead, I shoved aside a branch and gave grinning chase. I didn't call out, either, primarily because I felt sorry for the little girl; so quiet and gentle she was, and here she was dragged around like some kind of doll while her mother played this man against that, moved from this place to that . . . What kind of a life is that for a kid? Small wonder she wanted to play.

So I played with her.

After a few moments we were into an improvised running game of hide-and-seek. She would duck behind a trunk, I would creep up as loudly as I could and leap around it with a threatening grunt, only to find her darting away. She was fast, her arms catching shafts of sunlight like glints of warm steel; and more than once her energetic flailings would bring her perilously close to a fall on her face. Yet she never lost her balance. She pranced, she twirled, she wove across the hilltop like a zephyr seeking rhyme.

I tried to follow, but it wasn't long before I was feeling the pressure. Though the farther we ran the cooler it became, it was hard for my lungs to keep pace with my heart. Finally, calling out in laughing surrender, I sagged against a boulder and gulped for a breath.

She poked her head around a gnarled chestnut and grinned. I waved at her. She ducked back. And when I thought my legs could stand it I staggered after her. But she was gone.

A breeze came up, fluttering leaves and weeds.

She scrambled to the top of a flattened rock and put her hands on her hips. Grinned. A dart of sun caught her shoulder, and the violets still pinned there numbered just three.

I chased her, and she jumped silently down the other side. When I lunged around the rock, no more than five seconds behind, she had vanished.

The breeze to a wind. There were shadows of massing clouds that swept like wings over the woodland.

She popped up again, behind a brightly green laurel. And my vision was slightly blurred now, as if a glass had been set between us and had been coated with water.

"Hey!"

She didn't answer; she vanished.

We had already topped the summit and were making our way down the other side, an untouched stretch of woodland that spread to the flanking roads and would stop only when the first of the beyond-the-park estates threw up its stone wall. I was getting angry. She was making a fool of me, a mockery of the game, and if this was the way she was going to treat me when all I wanted to do was help and have some fun, she could take her goddamned violets and shove 'em down her throat. I considered leaving her then and heading back for her mother; surely the woman must be a panic by now. But it was easy to get lost in here, and she might come out on one of the roads and not know how to find her way back. It would serve her right, I thought then; the little bitch deserves a good scare.

"Hey!" It occurred to me suddenly that I didn't know her name. "Hey, Corey!"

A giggling. I looked up and saw her swinging from a low branch. I lurched into a run and she dropped instantly behind a bush. When I charged through it, hands outstretched, she had moved to another rock. Another tree. I felt as if I were struggling through air turned viscous, though my brain kept telling me I was moving at normal speed.

Leaves kicked into my face.

A giggling.

She was there on my right when I whirled around, there behind me when my eyes couldn't find her.

It was cold. Wind, shade, the touch of the ground and the brush of the shrubs.

I wanted to stop, but she was *there* on my left, and over *there* in a shimmering of stormlike grey. Ahead of me now, just within reach; and gone . . . always gone when my fingers reached for her neck, punched toward her shoulder, clawed for her eyes.

She was there, and she was grinning. God *damn* her for grinning!

There. Over there.

Grinning, always grinning.

And gone.

I couldn't find her. I staggered around in an erratic circle and couldn't find her. I swallowed, hugged myself, imagined myself slipping a hand around her throat and bulging her eyes, blackening her tongue. I shuddered violently, and the sensation passed as quickly as it had come. Gasping, then, I surrendered; she may have thought it great fun to tease the restaurant man into exhaustion and a fit of unreasoning anger, but I had other plans for the day, and they did not include strangling bitchy little girls or dying of exposure. But before I could take my first step back up the slope it started to rain—a slashing, sheeting rain that had me drenched within seconds. It was dark, almost twilight at two hours past noon, and though I didn't want to do it I began retracing my steps up the hill without the girl. A lesson if she got lost, I thought bitterly; a lesson not to take advantage of her elders.

I kept telling myself that when I finally reached my weeping elm and discovered Elizabeth gone. Great, I told myself with a punch at the tree; that's just . . . great.

With hands on my hips I staggered down the slope toward the gazebo. The musicians were putting away their instruments, and the crowd had already scattered. As I came up to Patrick Jameson, the postmaster and band leader, I managed to tell him between gulps and groans how much I'd enjoyed the medley. "To be honest," I said, "I never thought you guys would be able to handle stuff like that so well. I'm really impressed. You outdid yourselves today."

He looked at me oddly, lifted a page of sheet music from a stand and stared at it, back to me with a curious squint. "What in hell's so hard about Sousa, Tom?" he said.

I gaped, cleared my throat, wiped a hand over my face and finally shook my head.

"Must be the pond water," he said, smiling knowingly.

"What?"

"You're soaked, in case you hadn't noticed, friend. You find a little cutie in the water?"

I looked at him, hard. At the ground—dust, dry grass, a haze in the air. The sky was blue, the sun furnace-white.

"Yeah," I said. "You should've seen her."

It was the heat, of course, and not just the day of it but the week of it. Sullen, enervating, a presence unmoved even after the light was gone, it caused the mind to stagger, to lurch from one thought to another without the grace of reason. And it combined with one's emotional state into a practical joke that had no idea at all where mirth ended and pain began. I should have recognized the symptoms from the beginning; god knows, they were familiar enough from my days on the beat when shadows in trees looked like trapped little children, and the instructions of the chief came out garbled and harsh.

As it was, I imagine I seemed rather clumsy and even drunk to poor Patrick. He was a fine man. He refused to allow Time to be his foe in spite of the years that had settled on his shoulders. And he refused to allow fools like me to spoil what had obviously been a fine day for him. He grinned at me, poked me, told me with my tin ear it was no wonder Gershwin sounded a lot like Sousa. And I accepted the ribbing because I deserved it.

It was the heat, and I wasn't thinking, and I was so pleased that he had driven me back to the real world that I promised him and his men a free round or two whenever they came to the Cock's Crow for lunch. Then I did what I should have done before: I hurried back to my car (noting as I did so that almost an hour had passed since the little girl had lost me) and took Park Street out past the cemetery to Hollander's set-back Dutch Colonial. All this nonsense about black eyes and desertions was beginning to sound as though my gal Sunday had left her little mining town in the West and had come East instead. Lies, deceptions, rivalries—the men I had been friends with were suddenly men I did not know.

I had almost worked myself up to a point of active disgust when the house itself interrupted me.

I made a slow U-turn and parked in front of it, glanced at similar homes to either side before slipping out from behind the wheel and making my way up to the front porch. All the windows I could see were solidly closed, and the bulky air-conditioning units I knew should have been there were gone. The door was ajar. And the ground damp. I did not look up to check the sky.

As before, I moved inside with a call—an angry one, this time—shivering as a breeze slipped past me and touched at the dust I saw in the middle of the central hallway, swirling it away as though it were a desert floor and not pegged oak. The air stifled. I felt as if I'd stepped wide-eyed into the middle of a dream. I did not call again, nor did I search all the rooms; and I did not pick up the shriveled violet I spotted near the stairs. As soon as I understood I was alone, not about to be joined by anything living, I retreated to the Hudson and drove off.

There had been a momentary temptation to ask questions of the neighbors, but it passed when I realized with a start, and a painful one at that, that I wasn't a cop any longer and had no authority to bother people about what was rapidly becoming an irritating fancy.

And that irritation must have brought a flush to my forehead and cheeks because, when I reached home, Grace was waiting for me on the stoop, and when she saw me climb out of the car she immediately threw up her hands and hurried inside. I had a spare bedroom on the second floor, carved out of an attic where I stored most of my books and old magazines. She had occasion to use it now and then for changing, especially into her hostess dress when a vagrant mood swept over me and I was in no shape to play the genial innkeeper for a while, if not longer. She didn't mind it; it meant a few extra dollars in her paycheck, a chance to needle me unmercifully, and offered her the hope that tonight might be the night when I finally stopped treating her like one of the boys. Only a handful of people knew of this arrangement; Righteous, because he wasn't blind, and Rex, Paul and Sandy, because to keep it from them would have made me feel guilty.

I didn't follow her up. I went directly into the kitchen, poured myself a full inch of bourbon and sat at the table with the ugly black telephone set between my hands. It made me nervous. I tried a little chiding to get myself to dial, but that didn't work. I could not help seeing Rex last Friday night, hearing Paul's voice this morning, watching the girl-child taunt me into exhaustion. I could barely touch the receiver; it was too much like the moment before a storm, when the air congealed and the wind died and all the lightning in the world waited to strike—that moment when nothing was as it appeared to be, when everything was wrong and you knew it and could do nothing about it.

It occurred to me that Elizabeth and that child had one hell of a walk from Rex's house to Paul's. From Paul's house to the park. From the park to . . .

I dialed.

Neither Hollander nor Stephenson answered.

I tried the school, the Chancellor Inn, the Town Hall, a few mutual acquaintances, the hospital, the library, even the train station, where I was told that no one had taken the express into Hartford, nor the locals to intervening communities. Finally, with a deep breath that did nothing to help my nerves, I called the police and had my first bit of luck: Abe Stockton was catching messages that shift. He, at least, knew I seldom got worked up over things immaterial. And after listening to me for several minutes he quite rightly informed me that nothing at all untoward had happened; rather, nothing alarming enough to call in the Marines.

I didn't tell him about the rain, or the grinning game in the woods.

"Since when have you been Lonelyhearts around here?" he asked me then.

"Since I stuck my nose in where it didn't belong," I said.

"God, you're a grump."

"I'm hot, I'm tired, and the day I transpose Gershwin for Sousa is the day I'd better check myself into a private home someplace."

"The heat, Tom it's the heat."

"Yeah."

"You take care."

A polite way of saying get the hell off the phone so the real trouble can start.

I nodded at the receiver and rang off, sat back in the chair and stared at the ceiling. I was feeling so confused now that my eyes wouldn't focus, and I didn't hear Grace come in until she'd spoken to me twice.

"Sandy called," she told me, heading for the refrigerator and my stock of iced water.

"Oh, beautiful. He's not coming in, right? Just what I need. Did he give an excuse? No, never mind—Marie's paining again, right? Damn."

She turned with a coy swirl of her dark green skirt, the ruffles of her white satin blouse veiling and exposing the push of her breasts. Her hair had been controlled mysteriously into something not quite a bun just above the nape, and a few untrapped wisps trapped enough of the sun's last light to stand out as though charged. And

I knew then as I watched her the difference between this woman and E. Corey: Elizabeth's beauty, if beauty it was, challenged the watcher to pinpoint the source; Grace, on the other hand, had an aura of absolute reality about her. Touch her and she giggled or winced or slapped your hand. I had the feeling if I'd tried to pinch Elizabeth she wouldn't even notice.

"No," Grace said. "It's not Marie he was talking about. It sounded to me like he's got a little something planned on the side."

"Sandy? Our Sandy? The one who cuts my liquor and thinks I don't notice? That Sandy?"

She nodded.

I shook my head. "Nope. Nope, never in a million years, Gracie. Never happen."

"I can only tell you what he sounded like, Tom." Then she stared at me for a disconcerting moment and asked if I'd had anything to eat today. I surprised myself by realizing that my lunch might as well have not been eaten at all, and I told her so. Immediately, she began slapping pots and pans around for a quick meal to tide me until I could get Righteous to do me one of his specials later in the evening.

And as she worked, I protested Sandy's infidelity. "Besides," I added, "this is his big night. He makes more in tips now than he does all week, almost. It's got to be that he had a fight with Marie. Again. It must have been a bad one, though, the worst yet. He wouldn't cheat her, though. Not him. He hasn't got the guts, much less the opportunity. That woman keeps a hold on him like nothing I've ever seen."

"Tom, I'm not arguing. I'm just telling you what—" She stopped, turned away from the stove and brandished a skillet at me. "What's going on?"

"What do you mean?"

"Thomas," she said, her voice lowering dangerously, "I'm not kidding. I was going to ask you later, but you should see the look on your face." She waited for me to respond, scowled when I didn't. "Listen, Harry Jackson called me today, just around noon. He said you weren't home, and he wanted to know if I knew where he could find Elizabeth Corey. What is it with those guys?" She set the skillet on a burner and adjusted the flame. Dusted her hands. Looked back at me sternly. "He made me curious, Tom. I called around after he hung up. You know, there isn't anyone in town, no one that I talked to, who's even heard of this woman. Her kid hasn't been registered in school and . . ." She lifted her hands in silent question.

I debated telling her what had happened, for some reason not wanting her to think I'd been working too hard and the heat had finally gotten me. That's all I would need—a mother hen who thought one of her chicks had suddenly gone addled. But I lost. My confusion was such that I couldn't even decide if this should be a secret or not. And so, between bites and swallows and a few of her whispered comments that were maddeningly neutral, I started with Hollander's call this morning and continued until the point when I found his home empty. No. It was deserted. As soon as I said that I knew it was right. Deserted. Neither Rex nor Paul had gone to some ludicrous rite of chivalry. They were gone. Their homes were abandoned, and when I looked up to Grace I knew she agreed.

Suddenly, the food lost all its flavor and I pushed the plate away, wishing I were a drunk so I could smother all this under a cloud of booze. "I should have gone to Paul's right away," I said angrily, punching at the table for the marvels of hindsight.

"He wouldn't have been there."

I didn't ask her how she knew; I only knew she was right.

Then I glanced at the clock and uttered a few choice oaths that didn't turn a hair on her head. It was nearing four and if we didn't hurry, Righteous would be pounding on the door, wanting to know at the top of his voice if we were opening today or moving to Boston. Grace, however, insisted we wash all the dishes first, and before the last ones were dried and stored she had convinced me to take the battered Hudson and do a little shopping around. Try Sandy, try the houses again, take a tour of the streets to see if I could find Elizabeth and her daughter.

"If they aren't staying anywhere," she said, "they have to show up sometime. And this time you can ask them just where Paul and Rex are."

"But what if they come here?"

"They aren't ax murderers, you know." She made a play at flexing her muscles. "And I ain't no chicken, either."

I couldn't laugh and she knew it, and she laid her hands on my shoulders and put her cheek to mine. "I wish I had an answer for you, Tom," she whispered.

I took hold of her waist. "So do I. And there's probably nothing wrong at all."

"I know."

She kissed me, pulled back and squinted. "You're a little frightened, aren't you."

"Yeah," I admitted. "But that isn't the worst part."

She nodded. She knew so much I almost crushed her in a hug that as it was left her breathless. Then I grabbed my jacket from the hall closet and was gone.

peekaboo

Paul's house seemed diminished, squalid. I didn't even bother to get out of the car.

i see you

I drove past the park, slowed opposite the gates, and tried to imagine Elizabeth and the child coming out, meeting Rex, seeing Rex play his role to the hilt and sweeping an arm around both to take them first to dinner, then into his home.

hey, tom, i'm in love

The car moved at a virtual crawl, and I kept one hand at the wheel, draped over the rim at the wrist, and the other on the doorframe. It was like the old days, I thought without a trace of nostalgia, back in the patrol car; the only things missing were the voices buzzing from the radio. I had to shake my head vigorously to rid my mind of the superimposition, to concentrate on what I was seeing instead of what something thought I should see.

I looked in the alleys between the houses, between the businesses on Centre Street; I looked around the corners of hedges, of porches, of low brick walls capped with sleeping felines and sluggish, barely moving birds. From the back all the women began to look like Elizabeth and all the children wore violets pinned to their shoulders. Twice I had motorists blare impatiently at me and swerve awkwardly around the Hudson with a shake of a fist; and twice I nearly struck dogs that had ambled off the curb.

The sun was still full, balancing on the horizon, yet

the day felt like a midnight that would not yield to dawn. A midnight in July when the heat refused to crawl back into the shadows, when the air stilled and the cicada buzzed, when sleep was impossible and moving around just as bad.

On impulse I took Williamston Pike out into the valley, thinking they might have headed for one of the farms out there. But I saw no one walking, no one running, nothing at all on the shoulder of the road.

At one point I stopped. Dead. In the middle of the road. Thinking that perhaps it was time for me to see one of those new mind doctors. After all, I told myself as I stared at the trees, what had really happened? Nothing. Just because people weren't in their homes when I called or stopped by, just because people knew the same people I did, just because . . . but there was Grace and the look she had given me. She was not a fanciful woman; she had anchors that kept her feet on the ground in the highest of winds, the most turbulent of storms. Yet she too sensed a curious (for want of a better word) force in motion here in the Station. A force that had been somehow generated and fed by Rex Stephenson and Paul Hollander and, for all I knew, Sandy Fielder, too. It did not make any difference to the most literal of minds that such forces, whatever they were and wherever they came from, did not exist and do not exist. That was not the point. It had happened, it had begun, and until I could prove to myself otherwise, I could not help but believe it was true.

Later, when I had Rex's explanation for his hysteria on the phone and Paul's explanation for the lie about Elizabeth's eye . . . then and only then would I be able to see the logical thread that connected them, the points where I missed my connections and thus conned myself into thinking I was dealing with . . . forces.

Later. Later, when the alarms I had developed during those years as a cop stopped their incessant, infernal, frightening clamor.

Later, I thought as I pulled into the train depot, got out and had myself a few gulps of tepid water from the platform fountain.

Later, I thought as I pulled into Stephenson's driveway and stopped with the motor still running in front of the house. I stared at it, daring me to tell me a secret, to give me a hint, to unearth me a clue. But the more I looked the more deserted it seemed, the more forlorn, the more . . . hollow.

And it was then that I knew there would be no later.

No rational explanations, no brilliant feats of logic.

there was no black eye, and the girl-child wore violets

But even within the realm of the impossible there had to be something, a connection to be made that I was still missing. Rex and Paul and possibly Sandy. Two bachelors and a married man, all three of them smitten by the beauty of a wraith. My fingers drummed on the steering wheel while I watched the still-open front door hold darkness inside. Three men. Three . . . lonely men; lonely in spite of the people they had around them, lonely, and vulnerable to whatever Elizabeth had offered them, and had withdrawn.

But why withdrawn? Had they each said something to her that had kindled her anger—or had they tried to put their hands on her and that had sparked some safety valve, some trigger, some barely hidden mechanism that turned her vengeful.

Harry Jackson, said Grace, had been looking for her,

too. And I supposed that if I knew him better I would find he was the same.

But damnit, I demanded silently, who the hell is she?

A shadow drifted over the sloped hood of the car, darkened the face of the house for an instant and was gone. I craned my neck awkwardly and looked up, saw a cloud, several, taking the last light from the sky. They were large and they were boiling, and I almost had the window rolled up before the first drop slapped into my face. The stirring of thunder. The elms down the drive gave a dead voice to the wind, a roaring above their crowns that soon funneled to the ground. Leaves in dervishes, scorpion twists, and I had just turned the vehicle around when the rainlashing began.

Hailstones that pounded, a thrumming that bellowed, and when I put a hand to the key to start the ignition my fingers curled away from a stinging bitter cold.

Lightning walked over Oxrun Station, and the light that it gave me was dead flat and white.

My hands rose to the steering wheel and I saw them trembling, and I no longer bothered to tell myself I was dreaming, it was the heat, I had heard Gershwin only in my mind. The absolute wrongness of it all had finally worked its way completely through, left its residue behind. It was all wrong, and it felt right, and before I knew it I was barreling down the street toward Sandy Fielder's home.

As I veered sharply into a lonely sidestreet, thumped to a stop at the curb and killed the engine, I allowed myself one small smile of satisfaction: the storm was a real one, not simply centered over any one house. All the streets, all the buildings, all the trees were getting drenched, and I saw with my own eyes a half dozen people racing for shelter with newspapers tended uselessly over their heads.

It was a small consolation.

Sandy's front door was open, and all the windows closed.

Prudence should have kept me in the car, should have had me restart the engine and drive straight to the police station, where I could have made so much noise that someone, anyone, would have come with me to find what I was sure would be inside that house. But prudence also told me that ravings about a woman who came out of the park and was strolling around the Station killing off my friends would only land me in a cell until Grace came to take me home, to tuck me in, to fill me with soothing nothings about the rights and wrongs of the world until I fell into a fitful sleep.

So I did then what I had not done since the day I left the force: I thumbed open the glove compartment and took out the oiled holster that held my revolver. I didn't bother to examine it and search for memories, nor did I bother to load it; the sight of that barrel poking toward your stomach is enough for most poeple to lose what lunch they'd had, anyway. I slipped it into my jacket pocket, slid across the seat and opened the door. A deep breath to brace myself against the cold of the rain, and I was out and running, tripping up the steps and onto the porch, where I leaned against the wall and waited until my heart caught up with me.

The streetlamps had been turned on, but all they did was turn the air to a faint fog, illuminate the rain to darting streaks of silver, make the gloom more intense as I blinked the water from my eyes and moved inside.

There was no entrance hall or foyer; I was on the extreme right of the living room, the archway to the dining room directly beside me. There was no one in either; magazines on end tables, a radio against the far wall, table setting in the dining room winking against the lightning. I walked slowly across the carpeting toward the radio, toward a doorway that, at a glance, was apparently Marie's bedroom. I could see a dresser, a chest of drawers, laced curtains on the rear window, the foot of the bed. I sniffed, my nose wrinkling against the clear scent of disinfectant, but when I stepped over the threshold there was no one inside. Only the bed, with rumpled sheets a faded, soiled white. The window was open slightly from the top, and a gust of wind pushed at the curtains, nudged the sheets, drifted to the floor a long streak of grey dust.

I closed my eyes tightly, backed out and walked into the dining room, into the kitchen behind it, where I found a chair kicked back against the fire-scorched edge of a porcelain stove. There was dust underneath the chair, and on the hard-cushioned seat. This time, however, I knelt down and put a finger on it. Coarse, thick, not dust at all. Ashes. And they were still warm.

I had almost decided to leave when I heard a faint thumping outside. Quickly, I moved to the window over the sink and parted the curtains there. It was Sandy; he was standing on the bottom step of the back porch, whirling around as though the rain were the most wonderful, most delightful thing that had ever happened to him. I smiled . . . and killed it the moment I caught a good look at his face.

His eyes were wide, his nostrils flaring, and the arms I had thought were thrown up in pure joy were actually warding off some attacker I couldn't see. I rushed to the door and flung it open, just in time to see him leap to the ground and sprint across the back yard. I have no idea where he thought he was running to, but he never made it; a shearing wind slammed into him and toppled him, dropping him to his knees, where he stayed for a second, another, before looking up toward the back. Then the air split with thunder, and a glare of blue-white made me turn my head away.

But not before I saw it, the lightning that moved so interminably slowly that a crawling baby could have escaped it. A baby, but not Sandy. He was struck in the center of his spine, and his head snapped up, his mouth open in a scream drowned by the rain. Then he shuddered, slumped, fell prone to the ground.

I couldn't move. There was no question he was dead, had been the instant he'd been touched by the whitefire. Yet still I couldn't move to kneel beside him, to check him. Because, while I watched, streams of fog lifted from beneath him, his clothes burst into flame, and in the pouring rain he was transformed into ashes. Into dust. And despite the rain, and the nausea that was launching itself from every corner of my stomach, and the cry that had somehow become trapped in my throat, I could see quite clearly the space where his left hand had been, and I could see quite clearly the shriveled blackened violet.

How fast she moves, I thought as I stumbled back through the house: from the park to Paul's and now here to Sandy's. How fast she moves when she doesn't have a car. I had better tell Grace about how fast she moves. Suppose she wants to come to the roadhouse again? I won't have to give her a lift, of course. She moves fast. Without a car. She must carry the child under her arms, unless the child runs with her, so terribly fast that no one can see them, thinks they're nothing but the breath of a wind.

I sat behind the wheel listening to my mind babbling, waiting for it to catch up with the reality of what I'd seen. It was as though there were two people in the car: one was drooling slightly from the corner of his mouth, trying to force away the image of a man not burned but seared to death, trying not to imagine the way the lightning crept through the house to strike Marie in her bed and the boy in his chair, trying not to imagine what Sandy had said to Elizabeth and the child that made Elizabeth strike out with such indiscriminate fury; and the other, a saner, more rational creature not quite a man, waiting, just waiting, as though he had run a mile ahead and was resting while the rest of the pack caught up with his distance. Waiting. Just waiting.

Then I heard a clicking. Rhythmic, pulsing, filling the car until the storm was blotted out. I looked down and to my right, and saw that I had taken out the gun and was pulling the trigger. Again, and again, and again, and again, until I could feel the cramp begin to pull in my hand. It took most of my strength to pry the gun loose, and more to grab hold of the steering wheel once the engine had started.

It occurred to me then that I ought to call Harry Jackson, to warn him away from Elizabeth before she gave him a flower. But the only thing that was working for me was the part of my mind that told me to go home. The thought about Jackson vanished, and I pulled away from the curb.

There's no sense attempting to explain the convulsions I suffered during the next two hours. I can only
remember fragments of the drive, moments of rain, the
grumblings of the storm. I can barely remember pulling
up in front of my house and staggering inside, where I
found the bottle of bourbon still on the kitchen table. I
was tempted to drink without a glass, but caution somehow managed to get the first hold. I poured. I drank. I
poured again, ran into the bathroom and vomited.
Washed my face and poured a third time. Now the
liquor stayed, and the cold from the storm drained off
and was gone.

I returned to the bathroom and stripped. Showered.
Toweled dry as roughly as I could. By the time I had
dressed and was ready to face the roadhouse I had
caught up with myself, and I knew with a sickening
certainty that it was, at last, over. If Jackson was so
eager to get hold of Elizabeth, it meant that she had
somehow latched on to him during the previous night,
or perhaps this morning. And if she had, if she had
taken him as she had taken Rex and Paul and miserable
little Sandy, then it was fairly certain she had given him
the last flower. And as horrid as that made me feel, I
knew too there was nothing I could do about it. The
first time he angered her he was a dead man. It was as
simple and as horrifying as that. A dead man. A dead
man.

I walked around the house, then, for yet another
hour. I was attempting to convince myself that I was in
no danger. That there was no reason for me to try
Stockton again and tell him my story. Four flowers,
four deaths, and Elizabeth and the girl-child would walk
back into the park.

Oddly enough, my biggest problem was how to tell Grace. I could picture her sitting in her regular place at the bar, her hair in its twirl, her blouse with its ruffles, her face with that curiously amused, intent look. I could hear her asking me what I thought Elizabeth was, and I could hear me saying that she was a spirit of some kind. Maybe, if such things existed, an extension of a sprite, a faerie . . . though that last rang hollow since all that I'd read of faeries and their realm had been things of gentle, almost other-worldly beauty. What cruelty invaded it came from the land of men, not from themselves. But it was a thought, I could hear myself telling her; a thought better than nothing at all, since I had nothing at all on which to base my speculations.

Nothing, I thought sourly, but the dustgraves of five people.

Finally, close to ten o'clock, I knew I was stalling. I grabbed a raincoat and raced across the ground to the roadhouse's back door. Righteous was sitting on a stool near one of the ovens, his back to me, his hands holding a magazine whose contents must have been infinitely more interesting than my entrance since he didn't look up once, not even when I spoke his name in greeting.

In front the place was nearly empty. The storm and its abrupt rising had, as storms usually do, taken its toll on the voice of my cash register. I didn't mind. I wasn't sure I would be able to pull off the innkeeper role with the aplomb it deserved, not after what I had just seen, what I had been forced to believe. And Grace, bless her heart, took one look at my face and didn't ask a single question. Instead, she motioned for the substitute bartender—Patrick Jameson, in fact—to bring me a drink and sat me on my seat where I could survey my domain.

And so the night passed.

Slowly, quietly, every few minutes dropping a word to Grace about what I had not found. As soon as the first word had come to my tongue I knew I couldn't tell her. If she believed me mad, I would not be able to withstand her pity; and if she believed me, I would not be able to stand her terror. So I mentioned that the houses were still empty, that Sandy seemed to have taken off with his family, and that I was probably going to catch pneumonia from the drenching I'd taken.

At the last, however, I found myself walking more and more frequently to the door, staring out at the parking lot and the woodland across the road. Looking. Waiting. Unable to shake the feeling that once Harry Jackson had been taken care of, Elizabeth and the child would come back here. Not necessarily to me, but to meet someone else. Anyone else. It apparently made no difference who it was.

And that, I discovered when the last customer had left and Grace and Patrick were cleaning up the mess, was the real horror of this nightmare turned real: there were no odd markings on the victims to sign them as prey, no ancient family curses, no deep personal secrets. The men who had been taken were lonely, nothing more. And in their loneliness they had tacitly or otherwise accepted Elizabeth's presence, and that acceptance, that willingness to shed the feeling of being lonely, was the trigger for the storm.

I turned away from the door. It was mad. I was mad. All this talk of faeries and curses and markings on victims . . . I almost sobbed in self-pity.

To die the way Sandy had was most definitely preferable to a dying of the mind.

Patrick left with Righteous.

Grace came up to me, her coat over her shoulders, and she kissed me. "You all right?"

"Yes, I think so."

"That talk we had before, it didn't bother you?"

I frowned. "Sure it bothered me." *You're really a cold fish, Paul had told me.* "I'm just not used to tailing after a jinx, you know. It's something I never learned on the job, and it sure as hell isn't something I expected to find here, of all places."

"All right, all right," she said. "You don't have to snap off my head."

"I'm sorry."

"See you Tuesday?"

I smiled, kissed her, watched her hunch her coat over her head and race for her car. It sputtered a few times, and I couldn't help grabbing the doorknob and thinking maybe I should ask her to stay with me. The Cock's Crow had suddenly grown too large and too empty, but by the time I had made up my mind she had left me. Once again, I thought, you have taken the bull by the horns, Thomas you ass. My hand reached for the outside lights . . . and froze.

Across Mainland Road, on the slightly sloped verge before the forest began, were two figures blurred by the rain. A tall one, a short one, standing there without cover, without coats, unaffected by the storm. Their faces were pale, their hands clasped, and there was no doubt at all who they were watching.

I backed away and stumbled into a table. I pushed at it, and kicked aside a chair. Shadows from the dim wall lights. Murmurings from the kitchen. A dripping from a faucet behind the bar. They were out there, framed by the door's center pane. They were watching, they were watching, and I didn't stop moving until I fell against a barseat that jabbed sharply into my spine. I spun around, hands out and ready to grab . . . and saw it.

In the middle of the bar.

A tiny fresh violet; violet number four.

I refuse to believe it even now. I have the Cock's Crow and the Hudson, I have my friends on the force and my friends in the schools, I have memories of Rex's poetry and memories of Paul's laugh; I have Grace, goddamnit, and there's no possible way one could say I was lonely. Being alone is not the same, being alone in my case is entirely by choice.

They step onto the road. Hand in hand. And there is thunder.

I make a fist of my right hand and smash the violet into a pulpy smear I wipe off with a rag. I pull from the back of the register drawer the handgun that Sandy kept there in case of trouble. This one is loaded, and I pull back the hammer and stare at the door.

Lonely? Sometimes, I suppose, but surely not enough to set off whatever moves them. They've made a mistake this time and there's no way to tell them; they've made a mistake, but now they've met someone who knows what they're doing. I have no idea if bullets will stop them, but in the form they've taken I refuse to see why not, especially since it's the only thing I have at the moment, the only way I can prove I'm not losing my mind. Aim . . . and shoot Elizabeth straight through the heart. I can do it. I'm an expert. Straight through the heart, just as easy as that. Then the little girl will start screaming and go back where she came from. I can't see the flaw, though there's a trembling in my arm.

But there is one, damnit. I can feel it. I know it. I can sense it on the back on my neck, like the prickling that tickles before the first drop of rain.

There's a flaw.

And I'm blind.

And the door opens, and I see it.

The little girl is grinning—*damn, she's always grinning!*—and she releases Elizabeth's hand . . . and I see it. Oh god, I see it.

It isn't Elizabeth; it's the girl. That sweet little girl with the sweet little smile. With the dark eyes and long lashes, with rounded pink knees. Elizabeth, whatever she is, is only the lure, and the girl is the trap that directs all the dying. And for no reason at all, then, I remember Rex, and his Shakespeare, and the story of Oberon and Bottom, and most of all . . . Puck. A faerie, perhaps, but look closely and you'll see a streak of mean there that is centuries wide and blooded deep red. A vicious, tearing streak that hides not well under the guise of a prank.

It's the girl. It's the girl.

And I can see in her eyes a sudden fear of the gun that aims at her head. What it will do to her I don't know, but I do know she fears it, that it will destroy her some-how. It's the time, then, and I'm ready . . . it's the time when I'm ready to shoot down a little girl. A grinning little child. A gentle little child who played with me in the park, who sucked at her thumb, who looked at me with loving the way only a little girl can.

My god, it's the girl.

The lightning is coming.

I don't know if I can.

The black outside turns white, and shimmers.

I don't know if I can kill that little girl's smile.

If I do it, and I win, I know then I'll never see the sun bright again.

The windows all shatter, and the wind thrusts me back. My arm is up and aiming and . . . god, Tom, can't you see it's only a little girl?

A sweet little girl, a smiling little girl, a lovely little girl with a nosegay of fresh violets pinned to her shoulder . . . a nosegay of fresh violets too many to count.

PART III

Autumn, 1960

NIGHT'S
SWIFT DRAGONS

6:45 P.M.

The air was sharp, like the sudden snap of two fingers at memory's goad; the sun bled crimson to the tree-spiked horizon, and the shadows it cast were knife-edged and long. Foliage flared, and the few naked branches were jagged cracks in a sky that was cloudless and darkening. The streets throughout the Station were empty—a split second of desertion when all the pedestrians were still paused in doorways, and automobiles waited for the cold thrust of the key. On Centre Street a neon light was brittle and sputtering, buzzing like a summer fly trapped between two panes; on Devon a shutter banged, a wooden hand clapping for the onset of dusk; and on Fox Road a garbage can teetered at the edge of a cracked curb. There was no train at the depot, no movement in the park, and a crow by the hospital studied the remains of a long-dead squirrel.

The air was sharp, and the streetlamps winked on, doubling the shadows and multiplying the gloom.

The air was sharp, and it did not move.

A caught-breath silence that waited for a scream.

6:50 P.M.

The Oxrun Station branch of the Post Office was closed. Set back from Williamston Pike on the corner of

Centre Street across from the library, it accepted the
dusk as it had for a century—a dark-brick building with
broad and tall white-framed windows and a center-
peaked roof that spread to form perfect nesting eaves
for sparrows and grey doves. Four concrete steps edged
and split by a wrought-iron railing led to arched double
doors—one In, one Out—faceted perfectly into sixteen
small panes.

The lobby itself was building-wide, hushed, lighted
softly by four white globes on age-dark chains, globes
that served as graveyards for black-shadowed insects.
To the left of the entrance was an unmarked paneled
door with a brass knob unpolished by the touch of a
hand. Directly ahead, the lobby's rear wall was divided
into two unequal sections: the first—about ten feet
long—soared almost to the vaulted ceiling fourteen feet
above, was plain thick oak to the height of a man's
waist, frosted glass above that, and wood again to the
top. The glass was split into three brass-caged windows:
the first for stamps and special mailings, the second for
packages, the third for General Delivery and complaints
about the service. The remaining and largest portion of
the rear wall was a warren of glass-fronted, lettered and
numbered boxes, small ones on top, medium in the
middle, large along the bottom. All of them worked by
means of a key.

The rest of the lobby was a gleaming white marble
floor that was broken only by high tables with pens on
chains, stands for pamphlets, dampened sponges for
those who didn't trust their tongues.

There were faint cobwebs in the high corners.

There were echoes even at midnight.

Yet in spite of its austerity it was constantly filled with

voices, albeit voices that were subdued even when the lobby was filled to overflowing. The old men who met there to pick up their mail and plan their day always spoke in deferential whispers, as if aware of the dusty portraits of the five Presidents on the walls; mothers held their children in loose restraining grips to keep them from playing tap dancer between the legs of the grown-ups; and there was soft, constant chatter with the employees behind the cages—comments on the weather, on the upcoming presidential election, dollops of gossip for embroidery and expansion. Exclamations and explanations, however, were reserved for the library, the streets, and the autumn-chilled porches; here you were given only the icing, not the cake.

Behind the building was sanctuary—a small parking lot, and a concrete-aproned loading dock tipped with iron long since worn smooth by the soles of boots and the drop of mail sacks. Thick-boled trees cut sight and sound, visitors were unwelcome, and twilight came early no matter the season.

And no matter the season, Patrick Jameson always sat in his fan-backed wicker chair under the overhanging roof and waited for his postmen to return with the last pickup of the evening. He was alone. He enjoyed it. It provided him the first opportunity of the day to enjoy his cigar without someone grimacing at the aroma and making cracks about the ancient white holder he used to keep the tobacco away from his lips. He was a slight man even beneath the bulk of his blue windbreaker and white, roll-necked Irish sweater, his face not quite gaunt against the assault of sixty years. His hair was full and white and combed back in gentle waves from his forehead, his eyes large and brown, and when he spoke he used only one side of his mouth, as though he had been brushed by a stroke that had spared him for a while.

The sun bled lower and the air drifted to bronze.

A loud sigh of comfort, and he held the cigar away from his face and sniffed, catching the faint sent of burning leaves and smiling. This, he thought, was the most perfect of all seasons. More than a simple cleansing of the air, it was the absolute example of how to die right—in a blaze of unmatched color impossible to duplicate, complete with the distant cheers of a successful football game, the rush of automobiles from business to hearth, the giggling and snuggling under freshly aired blankets. Winter made you work too hard to get warm, spring was too tantalizing, summer too lazy. Autumn, on the other hand, was the unrepeatable blend.

A second sigh to underscore the comfort. Then he gazed over the lot and counted for the hundredth time the cars waiting there, their paint and windows hinting at the sheen of frost which would be born by morning. The green Studebaker Hawk belonged to Tony Winston, the youngest and most ambitious of his postmen; he, Patrick had decided sometime during August, would not last out the year, would succumb to the lure of higher-paying employment as soon as he figured out what he wanted from his life. The black Pontiac that should have died with the Korean War was Karen Redmond's, she of the sullen red hair and veil of pinprick freckles, with three kids and no husband and a figure that belonged in the middle of a cornfield. The '57 black-and-silver Chevy was polished three times a week by Harv Green, a compulsive janitor nearly Patrick's age who cleaned twice anything that didn't move out of his way. Harv was inside now, mopping down the lobby. The white DeSoto was Jack Fawn's.

And Patrick's eyes narrowed when he reached the back corner, under the hickory, where his own behemoth Caddy was parked, two spaces away from the nearest intruder. He hadn't really wanted to buy it, not at first; it seemed definitely too ostentatious for a mere postmaster to own. But Karen and Tony, their youth bubbling with fiscal mischief, had talked him into it in less than a week—with, admittedly, a little starry-eyed help from himself—using the argument that, without a family, a mortgage or backbreaking loans, why shouldn't he indulge himself before he was too old to enjoy it? Indeed. Why the hell not.

He grinned, examined what was left of the cigar, and glanced at his watch. It was just past seven, and Jack would be wheeling around the hospital to the mailbox there, Karen would be at the depot to pick up the evening drop and Tony would just be reaching the far end of Williamston Pike, out in the valley . . . if he hadn't stopped to gab with every woman along his route. Within the hour, then, all three would be back, the soiled grey sacks thrown onto the apron, a few words, a few quiet laughs, and he would be alone to begin the next day's sorting and put together the late-night pickup for the last train from the Station. They had all been after him to stop such extra work, even Jack of the sardonic grin and slick black hair; but he used the same argument they had thrown at him for the Caddy: without a family, not being much of a social drinker, no television, barely a reader at all . . . why rush home? Indeed. Why rush anywhere.

Excitement, by almost any definition, was not now, nor had it ever been, a part of his life. When he was young and craved it, it had avoided him, and as he grew older whatever sense of adventure he might have had was lost. Buried, perhaps. He was not at all sure. And the regrets he had had for such a sedentary life had long since given way to a grudging, automatic acceptance.

A quiet life. Small pleasures rather than avalanches that left behind them too much peace. Cumulative enough for late-night memories that eased him into sleep without too much of a pang. It was the way of things, he had taught himself. The way of things. Let the others have the adventures, then, and he would take the solitude. Besides being bad for the heart, excitement lent itself to letdowns, which were definitely not pre-scribed for a man living alone.

He sniffed loudly, pulled a handkerchief from his hip pocket and blew his nose. Then he shook his head at himself. He was listening to too much poetry on the radio or something; thoughts like that only led to stupidity, depressions and the wasting of hard-earned dollars.

And they also made his house too large.

He coughed, violently, and was glad for the noise.

He glanced up at the sky now streaking indigo and rose, straightening for a moment when he heard the sporadic cry of southward-bound Canadian geese. He could not see the flock as it passed over the Station, but it carried with it the one musical sound he had despised all his life—the sound of extreme loneliness uncurable, and loneliness unbidden.

A frown brushed his forehead, and he cocked his head slightly to one side. Though he could hear nothing once the geese had made their pass, there was another movement in the air very much like sound. Something not meant to be heard yet, and growing all the same. He strained and listened for several minutes, shrugged finally at the nudges of imagination and plucked the cigar from its holder, mashed it beneath his heel. His left hand immediately moved to his breast pocket, patting, but he checked himself just short of digging under the sweater. It would be a waste to light one now, when the others were due soon. A waste; like Stengel getting fired, and all that tax money going up into space for a bunch of tiny tin cans.

The frown reverted to his original tolerant grin. Crotchety is what Karen had told him he was, and even tire-waisted Harv had demanded to know if he couldn't honestly feel in the air what Senator Kennedy promised. Incredible. Harv pretending he was twenty again, back with the Marines massing under Old Glory. Harv-the-old-soldier spouting pie in the sky just because the young senator never wore a hat. He grunted a laugh and took hold of the lion's-paw armrests, shaking his head in slow amusement at the changes the world had seen since he had been born.

Not that Oxrun Station had changed all that much since he came into the world in the house out in the valley. A few stores switched owners, the Town Hall had been expensively refaced with brick and Italian marble, and there was talk now of tearing down the old library—a sister building to his own post office—and erecting something that, according to the Council, reflected contemporary society while, at the same time, kept within the bounds of good taste and Oxrun's appearance. And that, he thought sourly, was a damned contradiction in terms.

Then, aloud: "The hell with it." And he pulled out a fresh cigar. Lighted it defiantly. If the others objected, they could hold their damned noses.

7:25 P.M.

The heavy brown iron door to the loading bay slammed shut, and Patrick jumped, a hand to his chest, as he swore silently at Harv for unnerving him like that. The peace he nurtured, however, had been irreparably broken.

Almost before Harv had lumbered to the dock's edge the three post office trucks had lumbered down the narrow drive and into their slots. Engines coughed, a horn accidentally blared and the next fifteen minutes were spent hauling sacks indoors and hanging them from their square metal rigs for easy opening and refilling. Once done and time cards clocked out, Patrick led them all back outside, a ritual of departure for every day but Friday, when the weekend beckoned too strongly and amenities were postponed.

There was a momentary silence, then, and Patrick heard again the sound-not-a-sound approaching the Station. When he looked to the others, however, they seemed to notice nothing. It bothered him, and he scratched hard behind his right ear. It was late, he was tired, but nevertheless there was something . . .

He spat dryly and returned his attention to the others.

Jack Fawn, his face pocked from a severe adolescent dose of acne, stood on the ground combing his unkempt black hair and chiding Tony none too gently for the fresh scratches on his truck, no doubt caused, he said dryly, by Tony's tipping over fire hydrants in his frantic pursuit of skirts that never touched a knee. Harv and Karen stood by Patrick's chair, listening and saying nothing until Jack finally paused for a breath and Tony, flushing his impotent anger to a dull red on his cheeks, lifted a trembling fist.

"No," Patrick said wearily. He gestured toward the front with his dead cigar. "Later, yes, out in the street. Now, if you don't mind, no."

"Oh my, the man thinks he owns the place," Jack said to the air, lightly and without offense.

"The man, as you put it, is responsible for accidents and fights," Karen told him sharply, her voice just short of shrill. Her hair was cut short and brushed back over her ears as though she delighted in the boyish appearance it and her figure gave her. "You want to play hero, Jack, go to the park and pick on the little kids."

"O Lord, O Lord," Jack said in mock consternation, his gaze lifted to the stars, his hands at his chest in a parody of supplication.

"Jack!" she said.

He turned to her slowly, his hands lowering to his hips. He ducked his head a fraction and stared at her from beneath eyebrows that were broad slashes of black. "Hey," he said softly, "who the hell died and left you God?"

"No one, smartass."

"Hey," said Harv, waving a three-fingered hand impatiently, "knock it off, huh? This here's a lady, y'know?"

"Tell me another," Jack muttered.

"Damnit," Tony said then, stalking back to the dock, his thin arms stiff at his sides. "Damnit."

Patrick only closed his eyes and sighed to himself. He had hoped that his last year on the job would be filled with friendly bantering and gentle ribs that meant no offense, evenings on the dock watching the sun set, trading stories about the lunatics on the routes; instead, suddenly, what he was getting was internecine warfare, and it didn't take much imagination to see that he'd be out of three good workers before the month was out if this kept up.

But it would be too easy to blame it all on Jack. Though they did not find themselves compatible for anything more than a casual acquaintance, he could not help feeling a twinge of guilt whenever the younger man jumped on the others, as if the verbal abuse somehow had something to do with him. Not that he felt sorry for Fawn; lots of people, himself included, had no family, made little money, and just couldn't seem to find the right formula for getting by in the world. No, he didn't feel sorry for Jack at all; what he did feel was a curious regret that he had not been able to get through to the man. The other three had vulnerable spots they practically wore on their sleeves. Jack, however, had armored his thoroughly.

"Listen," he said then, and the others turned to him quickly. "Why don't you all just head on home, all right? You'll give an old man nightmares with all this bitching and moaning."

None of them moved. Faces were averted, shoes scuffed on the lot's blacktop. In the distance, a truck's horn, and the muffled shriek of a cat.

"Hey, Pat," Karen said quietly, "you ever miss the band and all?"

He shrugged. It was a question he heard twice a day,

every day, every damned week. And no matter how often he answered it, folks did not seem to want to believe him. "No," he said. "Not really."

"The Station's own Benny Goodman," Harv said with a clap to his shoulder. "You shouldn't have done it, Pat. You should've hung on."

"Why?"

"Well, because . . ." Harv twisted his bejowled face into a semblance of deep thought. "Because, that's why. It was your band, wasn't it?"

"No, Harv, it was the town's."

"But you were the only one who wanted to lead it. I mean, every Saturday June and July and August there you were in that red coat and your trombone and . . . and hell, you shouldn't have done it."

Tony sauntered over to the dock and leaned an elbow on it. "You did some good sounds, Pat."

Patrick shrugged again. Maybe he did, maybe he didn't. The band had been all volunteers, and they'd practiced throughout the spring to ready themselves for the weekly concerts. The Council, for years, had given him a grant for music and instruments—and lessons, where needed—but two years ago had decided to temporarily postpone the concerts for lack of funds. And that, the Station knew, was extraordinarily far from the truth. What it did not know, and what Patrick would not tell anyone, was that he had been tired of the grind. One morning he had gotten out of bed and had looked in the mirror and had seen sixty, seventy—eighty, if he were lucky—staring him in the face. And his life had become so predictable that he could have filled out a yearly calendar for a decade ahead. It wasn't the grind, he'd finally admitted, it was the apparent accuracy of the chart that showed him the rest of his life.

The band, then, was the first casualty.

The post office would be the second.

The only problem was, he still hadn't figured out what to do about the rest. He hated traveling, didn't know many women and certainly wasn't about to marry this late in life, would not go into politics on an overwhelming bet . . . and that left listening to goodhearted people like Karen and Harv telling him he should not have done it, not at all . . . not at all.

"Could've gone on Ed Sullivan," Jack mocked without turning around.

"Now that ain't fair!" Harv said.

"All right, all right," Patrick said wearily. "Why don't you people just go home and leave me alone."

They hesitated. He could sense them leaning toward their cars, thinking there was something they should say to make his evening more cheerful. Even Jack glanced at him sideways, warily, one hand lightly fingering the comb poking out of his hip pocket.

It was Tony who made the first move, and Tony who stopped suddenly and looked toward the drive at the side of the building. For a moment they watched him, puzzled; then Patrick heard the sound he'd been aware of since he'd first taken his chair.

A grumbling like thunder that has lost its timbre. A slow and steady shredding of October's night air.

A breeze gusted, and gold-red leaves fluttered down from the trees to dust the hood on Patrick's car, stark against the white finish and somehow obscene. The shadows merged to become twilight, and twilight filtered hazily into dusk, into a textured dark. In the eaves directly overhead was the intense, flat white glare of the building's night-light, and it bleached the color from their faces, life from their eyes, set them into razored relief against the background of the trees.

A grumbling like thunder that had snapped lightning's reins.

Swollen and unwavering, and without reverberation.

They listened without comment, frozen, curious, though Patrick could not help shuddering at a tremor of apprehension. His first impulse had been to label the sound the result of a truck lumbering in from the highway, or an automobile whose muffler had died. But a moment had scarcely passed before he knew he was wrong. And he refused to believe in the stench of premonition.

He was about to dismiss it, then, with a caustic remark about engines and Detroit when Tony suddenly took a step toward the drive. They all jerked their heads around toward him, waiting, until Jack waved him still with a hand-slash in the air. It was evident Tony was going to disobey him, but Jack motioned again, less harshly, and the grumbling grew to a bellow.

Patrick's holder disappeared into his pocket.

Karen's thin lower lip was gnawed at by her teeth.

Then Jaek, with a soft noise of disgust, vaulted in a single motion onto the dock and headed inside. The others followed without hestitating, Patrick trailing with one hand rubbing the back of his neck. They wove through the sorting bins and warrens and through the inside door into Patrick's front office. There was a single window facing Williamston Pike, tall and arched and gleaming from a recent washing, a dark-green shade pulled halfway down. A chipped wooden desk piled with forms, ladder-back chair that swiveled and a clanking, unpainted iron-coil radiator; a print of George Washington on the back wall; a radio with cloth grille and two knobs missing.

Patrick refused to look at any of it. He spent as little time in here as possible, preferring to work at a grey metal desk in back where he could gossip and joke with the women who worked here half-days at the windows and sorting warrens. The room reminded him of a closet, a closet newly emptied because its owner had died.

They gathered at the window, Patrick given the center without anyone objecting. The thunder was audible, giving a tremble to the wood flooring, clearer when Jack lifted the bottom sash and let the night-breeze inside.

Karen's hand touched his elbow, and he patted it absently, hoping his disapproving scowl would belie his jumping nerves.

"I seen a movie once, you know," Harv said, barely above a gravelly whisper. "These guys they come into this little town—out in California, I think it was; yeah, California—they come into this town and they take over, you know what I mean? They come in like they was some kind of gods and they do all kinds of—"

"Yeah, yeah," said Jack impatiently. "We all saw it a million damned times, Harvey." He leaned heavily against the window frame to Patrick's right, his left hand grabbing at the point of his collar. "We all saw it."

"Yeah?"

"Yeah."

Patrick did not know what they were talking about. At the moment he did not much care about references to movies. The thunder was beginning to sort itself into abrasive noise, and he was angry that his perfect season was being so rudely interrupted.

He also did not like the moisture breaking on his palms.

But he said nothing when Karen switched off the office lamp and reached around the jamb to extinguish the lobby globes as well.

8:10 P.M.

Buried deep in the foliage of the curbside trees there should have been a streetlamp burning; a week ago, however, the bulb had been shattered by a stone and uncharacteristically not replaced immediately after the breakage had been reported. The nearest light, then, was across the Pike and nearly thirty yards down, its weak white cast jigsawed by leaves and drained by distance. No cars headed in or out of the village, no buses, no trucks. The sidewalk was deserted.

And they came down the center of Williamston Pike as though the road had been created expressly for their passing.

They wore black caps banded down in the center to give a rise to unemblemed peaks. Their jackets were leather, black, broken by the slanted death's-head grins of a dozen glittering zippers on breasts and sleeves. Trousers black. Wrapped about at the cuffs and tucked into heavy black boots studded with chrome points. Beneath them, Harleys black and chrome.

They rode slowly, three pairs and a leader, their black vanishing into the background of virtually full night, their chrome catching the streetlamps and throwing back lances.

Sexless.

There was no visible signal; directly in front of the building they wheeled and cut their engines, rolling silently to the curb, facing the doors, legs out for balance. No insignia glared from jackets or bikes, and their faces were hidden in the dusk of their caps.

The thunder/noise faded.

They waited.

They watched.

8:20 P.M.

"I don't know why everyone's so worried," Karen said. They had given up watching the bikers and had scattered themselves around the small office, pulling in chairs from the back room but refusing to call from the window or turn on the light. "They're nothing but some punks looking for trouble. As soon as a patrol car comes by they'll leave." She had opened the top two buttons of her shirt, and the pale flesh exposed almost glowed. "This is silly."

"You think they'll shoot us or something?" Harv asked fearfully.

"Let 'em try," Tony said, pacing in front of the window. "Stupid jerks must think this is a bank."

"It's how they get their kicks," Karen said from the corner. She shook her head vigorously to drive hair from her eyes. "I read about it in the *Reader's Digest*. They like to pick out a small place and make a lot of noise, stuff like that, get the people so nervous they do anything they want. It's the bikes, you see. All that noise. And wearing black like that, it's like the bad guys in the movies. If you ignore them, they go away."

"Just like bullies," Jack said, his tone flat.

"Right. When . . . well, there was this one gang, they went into a town in Oregon, you see, and the people there they wouldn't pay any attention to them. So they started breaking things, and the people still wouldn't mind them. So they went to this diner to beat up on somebody just to show the town they were in big trouble, and it was filled with cops. Every one of them ended up in jail." She smiled brightly. "All we have to do is wait for the cops."

"Just like that," Jack said.

Karen frowned. "Why are you talking like that? If you're so scared of them, why don't you leave?"

Jack turned away from the window, but he said nothing.

"War of nerves, right?" Tony said to Karen. When she nodded, he grinned eagerly. "Yeah, right. They think they've got us, but all we have to do is—"

"Wait for the cops," Karen finished for him, as though it were a lesson he should have learned the first time she'd said it.

Tony stood beside Jack and looked out. "Sure are big, though."

"It's the clothes and the bikes," Karen told him. "And it's dark. They always work better in the dark."

"You seem to know an awful lot about bike gangs," Jack said. He had returned to the window, his right hand tracing the outline of the several small panes.

"I told you, I read it—"

"I know," he said.

Tony took a step toward the lobby door. "I think maybe we should go out—"

"No!" Jack did not move, but Tony spun around as

though his shoulder had been grabbed. Harv, seated behind the desk, watched wide-eyed. "No. Like . . . like
Karen says, leave 'em alone."

Tony hesitated, then nodded, reluctantly. "I guess."

Patrick moved into the back room. He had been
listening to Karen, to Jack, had heard things there he
didn't like: Jack was trying to be too unconcerned, and
Karen was barely able to suppress the panic he detected
at the edge of her voice. She was most likely thinking
about her children, he decided; they were all teenagers,
overly protected, and tended to bust loose whenever she
wasn't around to handle the whip. Good kids, though.
They all had jobs after school, all did their homework,
were all hoping for scholarships to put them through
college. At the same time, he recalled a weekend last
summer when they'd smuggled beer into their rooms
while Karen had been out on a date, and once roaring
drunk they'd nearly destroyed the house. Patrick was
glad he hadn't been there when Karen had come home;
the neighborhood said the yelling didn't stop until
dawn.

Absently, he paused in front of one of the sorting
warrens and reached into a mail sack. His gaze touched
on an address and his hand moved automatically. It was
five minutes before he realized what he was doing,
another full minute before he could tear himself away
and walk to the back door. He took hold of the cold
metal bar, but did not push down. He was surprised
none of the others had come back here; it would be easy
enough to slip out the back, through the trees to the next
street and get hold of someone or head right down for
the police. Instead, they'd all remained by the window,
watching the bikers, bickering, pontificating . . . as

though they did not want to know if there were any more in the parking lot.

He did, however. He had no intention of allowing a bunch of young idiots to ruin his evening. And once it became clear the others were just as fascinated by the tableau outside as the bikers seemed to be by the post office, he couldn't help a loud snort of disgust. No one heard him. And now he hesitated with his hand on the bar.

"Fool," he muttered to himself. And pushed. And stepped back with a frown when the bar would not move. He blinked rapidly, moved forward again and pushed. The bar still would not move; the door was locked from the outside. And that, he knew, was impossible. In his pocket was a large key ring, and on that ring was the only key to the building's doors; not even old Harv had been granted the trust to lock up when the day was done.

"Something the matter?"

He almost sagged against the door, a curse lodged in his throat. Tony reached around him and tried the bar, scowled when it wouldn't budge, swore when his full weight only made his feet slip on the concrete floor. His face dropped a few years and became etched with apprehension. "I don't get it, Pat. This can't . . . I don't get it."

Patrick pulled out the key ring and stared at it, examining, hoping to discover that the proper key had been dropped, had slipped off and was gone. But there it was—the large green one polished smooth by his thumb. "Neither do I."

Tony kicked at the door's base, jammed his hands into his pockets. "Maybe they got something against it, y'know?''

"Are there still seven out there?''

Tony nodded.

"Then they haven't had time to come around back.''

"There must be more of them, then.'' But the young man's voice was weak, knowing it disbelieved. "How'd they do it, Pat?''

Two lights only illuminated the back room: one just above them, naked from a fraying wire; another over by the chipped door to the restroom, a wire cage protecting it and smearing its glow. Patrick glanced around at the shadows and considered switching on the green-shaded lamps on his desk here, and over the pigeonhole blocks set on wooden tables where the sorting was done. Then he glanced to the front and decided he didn't want any more light showing than was necessary . . . not until he better understood what was going on.

Tony pushed at the door a final time and glared at Patrick, who brushed past him suddenly and hurried back to the office. Karen interrupted a discussion of bike gangs with Harv when he entered. He did not look at them. He stood in front of the door to the lobby, wiping his hands on his trousers before grabbing hold of the bolt and shoving it back. The brass knob was cold in his palm, rough-edged, turning only after he had exerted more pressure than he thought he should have.

The lobby was shadow-streaked, gloomy, the high ceiling buried in a black nightcloud. Tony followed him as he walked to the front doors.

"Pat, you're not going out there!''

There was a cold in the room. It penetrated the thick rubber soles of his shoes; it slipped down the walls; it gathered under the ceiling and fell like drizzle on his shoulders. He reached out a hand toward the door, stopped, walked over to the nearest radiator and touched it. It was cold. He looked at Tony, who was baffled into scratching his head, and returned to the doors. Sixteen panes in each, and the bikers were watching.

"Pat?"

"If you want," he said hoarsely, "you can pull down the shades a little."

Tony grabbed the task gratefully, reaching up for the rings while trying not to expose himself, pulling the green shades down a pane more than halfway. While he did, Patrick, pushed at the right-hand door—it swung away from him easily; he pushed at the left—it creaked, but it moved.

There was a window in the bathroom.

"Hey, Pat, I—"

He ignored Karen's rising from her chair and took the distance to the restroom without knowing he was moving. Inside, over the basin, the frosted window was closed. He reached up and pushed, grunted, pushed harder . . . knowing it usually only took a fingertip to move it.

Voices in the office filtered back to him. He shook them off and reached down for the wastebin under the basin. It was half filled with brown, coarse paper towels, and he dumped them onto the tiled floor, heaved the basket to his shoulder and rammed its bottom rim against the glass. Twice more before he told himself it wasn't going to break.

He had no idea when he had started to perspire, nor how long he had been gaping at the window, but he was snapped out of his stupor when he heard Karen shouting. Virtually at a run, then, he headed for the office, just in time to see Harv lift himself from behind the desk.

"Tony," the old man said, pointing with his maimed hand.

Patrick swerved into the office, and threw up his hands to catch Jack, who had been flung backward somehow. Karen was holding onto the windowsill to the right of the door. The door itself was just swinging shut.

"Jackass," Fawn said, untangling himself from Patrick's reluctant grip.

Patrick ran for the door.

"Pat, no!" It was Karen.

He watched Tony taking the steps to the walk at a jump, his left arm raised in angry gesticulation, his right hand brought to a fist by his chest. He was headed directly for the bikers' leader, shaking his head, pointing back to the building, his whole attitude a demand for some kind of explanation.

The riders did not move. Chrome glinted, and their faces were still hidden.

Patrick reached for the brass plate to open the door, caught himself just as Tony halted. There was something about the way he held himself, a sudden stiffening of his spine, a slight tilting of his head. Then, before Patrick could say or do anything, Tony whirled around as though he'd been slapped. His hands were scrabbling at his throat, his dark eyes bulged in horrified disbelief, and from his nostrils poured twin streams of blood that looked black. His mouth opened, lips drawn tight, and there was blood like drool sweeping over his stained teeth. He staggered toward the steps, and his eyes began bleeding. He fell hard to his knees, one hand outstretched in clawed supplication, and his head snapped back as if he had been slammed under his chin.

His head snapped back, neck flesh tore blackly; his head snapped back . . . and kept on going.

Bounced. Rolled. Came to a rest against the leader's front wheel . . . facing the building . . . staring at Patrick with bloodbright eyes.

Karen dropped to the floor and vomited.

Tony's body sagged onto the steps, his hand still clawing for the safety of the doors.

Patrick did not move until Jack Fawn touched his arm.

"My god," Patrick said numbly, his eyes searching Jack's face for a sign of explanation. "My god, they shot him."

"Really," said Jack, leading him to the office. "I didn't hear a thing."

9:20 P.M.

Harv slumped against the back door, his massive chest swelling as his lungs struggled for air.

"I saw it," he said, though there was no one near him. "I saw it. Guam. This shavetail, punk Point lieutenant, he said we had just two hours to make a move or we'd be run over. He was standing there bold as brass, two seconds later he was . . . gone. I saw it. Honest to god, I saw it."

He held up his hand and stared at the stumps of his fingers. He smiled. Looked up when Patrick walked by.

"I used to tell the kids they came out at night," he said, nodding toward his hand. "Like some kind of flowers." He stared at the hand, at the deep red blotches and the pinpricks of red. He remembered then that he had been pounding at the iron door. "I saw it. I really saw it. One minute he was there, the next minute he didn't have a head and I almost didn't have a stupid hand. Two more feet and I would have been dead. Two more feet. Like night flowers, Pat." He grinned, sobered, looked at his hand. "What the hell are they?" he whispered to the stumps.

"You know something, Pat? Tony, he was always asking me if he could date Missy. She's my eldest. You remember her, don't you? Red hair like me, but better taste in men. Funny, but I'm only thirty-three and I already got a daughter who's seventeen. That's what you get for being a child bride, I guess. Of course, you wouldn't know about that, would you, Pat, living all alone the way you do. I don't understand it, really. You're not a bad-looking man even now. Don't get me wrong, I didn't mean it to sound bad like that. But you must have been damned handsome when you were my age. You should have married, Pat. You should have had kids like mine. They're beautiful. They get into trouble once in a while—remember that beer thing last summer? —but they're really good kids. I'd sell myself on street corners to get them to college, I really would. They're not like their father at all. He was good-looking, but he always went off someplace every month or so. To have some fun, he said. To get women, I knew. But it was fun for a while. We laughed, we traveled—have you ever been to Washington? The state, I mean. Beautiful. Really beautiful. Or Texas? God, we traveled, Pat. Then the money ran out and so did he. But he left me three damned fine kids, Pat, and don't you forget it. Please. Don't forget my kids. You don't have any of your own, so don't forget mine. Please?''

Jack lowered the receiver just as Patrick came into the office. "Not even a dial tone," he said.

Thirty minutes after Tony died and Karen had stopped screaming and Harv had dropped to the floor to babble about the Army and his days in Korea, Patrick stopped his pacing back and forth across the lobby. It was morbid, it was most probably sick, but he could not help moving to the window every few minutes to stare out at Tony's body. At the hand lifting above the steps. At the head. At the blood. It fascinated him, and it revolted him, and he cursed himself in every way he knew for wondering how it had felt, what it had been like.

Senility, he thought; senility brought on by shock.

He walked down to the boxes and stared through the windows. They were all empty. No circulars, no letters, no small pink slips that signaled a package. He trailed a hand over one of them, then fell back into the corner and crossed his arms over his chest. There was no time left to delay; he could no longer deny that what was happening was real. There'd always been that hope, of course, when he'd found the back door locked. And the bikers could have been just as Karen said—punks out for a thrill, like those Hell's Angels he'd heard about from the West Coast.

But that had all changed with Tony's death.

He played it back several times in his mind and knew Jack had been right: no shot had been fired. The riders had sat there with hands gripping the handlebars, faces hidden in the dark . . . and Tony had somehow been ripped apart.

It was real. From the silent scream to the silent prayer to the blood blackening on the concrete. It was real. Just as being unable to leave the back way was real; just as being unable to smash the restroom window was real; just as the telephone going dead was real. Was real.

There was no waking up from what he did not understand.

He jammed a cigar into the holder and lighted it. Drew on it. Without debate placed the orange-glow tip against the inside of his wrist and grimaced at the hiss of burnt flesh and greying hair. And it made him think of what a dragon could do.

All right, then, he thought as he blew on the blister. All right.

He looked up and saw Jack standing in the office doorway. A solid black outlined against the glow of the tiny lamp turned on at the desk. A question stopped itself as his lips began to move. Now wasn't the time. Jack knew, but now wasn't the time because Patrick wasn't quite positive he could handle the answer.

On the other side of the glass-and-wood partition he could hear Karen weeping, hear Harv trying to comfort her, hear the tap in the restroom dripping arhythmically.

Then he thought he heard Jack mutter: "They used to be horses."

10:10 P.M.

It was full dark in the Station, but the riders could be seen clearly.

And not once had a car passed in either direction.

10:45 P.M.

It occurred to Patrick that not since the bikes' thunder had died had he heard a single noise from the outside. No birds, no motors, no insects, no wind. He took a careful deep breath and held it, felt his pulse race in his throat, then walked slowly to the back room to bring the others into his office.

Only Jack met his gaze, and Patrick looked away quickly.

Five minutes later they were settled, the small lamp switched on and the shade drawn to the sill. It did no good, however; the light was dim, bouncing off the desktop to form shadows under their eyes, and none of them could resist a glance at the window every few minutes. The only sound was their breathing.

Patrick sat behind the desk and rubbed his palms hard over his face from forehead to chin. His vision was beginning to blur, and though he had taken four glasses of water in the last half hour his mouth felt as if it had been packed with cotton. When he cleared his throat, Karen snapped a hand to her neck, smiling weakly, foolishly, while Harv moved to stand behind her and lay a palm on her shoulder.

"Before anyone says anything," Patrick said then, astounded that his voice betrayed none of his apprehension, "I want you all to understand that what we're doing here is real." He held up the wrist with the cigar burn. "It's real, no matter how insane it may seem. Just don't ask me what it is because I don't know."

"It's a dream," Karen said, ignoring what he'd told her. "I'm sure of it. See, I was reading in the *Reader's Digest* about dreams and things like that, and they said that you can have a dream that's so real you can't tell the difference between your sleeping and your walking around. You can even tell yourself it's a dream and you won't believe it as long as you're dreaming." She stopped, frowning to herself. "Does that make sense?"

"It does to me," said Harv, "but who's doing the dreaming?"

"I am," she told him. "See, I'm having this dream and you're all in it."

"Then how come I can think?"

"You only think you can, but you can't, not really. It's all me, you see. Everything that happens is because of me." She smiled brightly. "And as long as I stay inside here, nothing's going to happen."

"Where are you sleeping?" Jack asked, disbelief apparent.

"Home, where else? The day ended, I drove home, probably fell asleep on the couch the way I do sometimes, and . . ." She spread her arms to finish the thought. Then: "I just wish it wasn't so damned scary."

Patrick had covered his eyes with the heels of his hands while she talked, grinding pain into his mind to keep himself from believing such a seductive explanation.

"We could all be crazy, you know," Harv said then, moving away from Karen's chair to the middle of the room. "I saw a movie once, these people were all in this cave, see, and they couldn't get out. So one by one they started to go crazy, seeing things that weren't there. Some guy turned into a monster, but he didn't, really. It was just that the other crazies thought he had, so they killed him. And when he was dead he changed back and they knew what they'd done. But they was still all crazy."

"What happened at the end," Jack said in the middle of a sigh.

Harv looked sheepish. "I don't know. I fell asleep."

A silence prolonged, and Patrick lowered his hands to find them watching him. Slowly, sadly, he shook his head. "It's nice to think that," he said, "but . . ." He shook his head again.

Suddenly, Harv jerked his head around and stared at the shade.

"What?" Patrick said.

Harv shrugged. "Don't know. I thought I heard my name."

"You're crazy," Jack said, smiled quickly, and Harv laughed.

Karen leaned forward to the edge of her chair. "If this is . . . if it's right, Pat, then who are they out there?"

"I don't know."

"Demons," Harv said, though he looked at nothing but the breeze-stirred shade. "There was this movie about them. They come from the devil and they do really rotten things to people because they sold their souls to the Devil."

"What have you sold besides stamps," Patrick demanded.

"It was just a thought," Harv said.

A thought to pass the time away, he decided, seeing that talking was better than just sitting . . . or trying to break through something that would not shatter. And if they talked long enough, loud enough, even stupidly enough they might even hit upon the reason for their being tormented this way. He glanced at Jack and received neither encouragement nor support. The man simply stood by the window and stared pensively into the corner. Again he could not help the feeling that Fawn knew more than he was saying—which was nothing at all aside from skewering opinions—and again did not want to know if the man knew anything at all.

He folded his hands in front of him and nodded. "The way I see it," he said, "these . . . whatever the hell they are out there, they're not perfect. Even those demons, Harv, weren't perfect: there were ways to beat them at their own game."

"What are you going to do," Jack said. "Play the trombone at them? Joshua at the gates of the United States Post Office?"

"Shut up, Jack!" Karen said. "At least he's trying."

Jack subsided into a corner, a shadow in shadowland that waited for its summons.

"Go on," she urged gently.

Patrick nodded, but allowed himself a moment for his strength to return. This was insane, he told himself; you're an old man, for god's sake, not the damned general of a fort.

"What I meant was," he said at last, "is that they're after something. I don't believe in coincidence. They're after something that's right here in the building." His tongue touched at his lips. "One of us, maybe, or something that belongs to them that's here in the mails."

"We can't open the mail," Harv protested. "Pat, that's against the law!"

"I didn't say anything about opening the mail. I was just making a suggestion."

"A good thing, 'cause I don't want any part of it."

"Harvey, please, just let me finish." He took a deep breath, sniffed, exhaled. "The point is, like I said before, they're not perfect. That means they can be beaten. What we have to do is study them, find out something about them and use it against them." Karen opened her mouth to interrupt, but he closed it with a wave. "No," he said, anticipating. "We haven't really studied them. We've been just looking at them. "There's a difference."

"I must say, you're talking about this as though it were like a problem in math," Karen said. Her face had gone pale again, and her lower lip trembled.

He wanted to tell her that he had to. If he fell into the panic boiling somewhere inside him, he knew he would never climb out sane. He had to force himself to treat this as if it were little more than an ordinary problem, one that obeyed all the rules of logic and reason, no matter how illogical and unreasonable it seemed at the time. He had to. There was no question that he had to. It was bad enough dealing with his own fear; he didn't want to have to carry the others' as well.

"So?" Harv looked at him hard; then, without waiting for an answer, he strode to the window and yanked up the shade. His hands gripped the sill. His head jutted forward and his shoulders were squared. "Bastard." He snapped around and glared at them. "That's what they are, y'know. Punks. Creeps. They think they can come into my place and take over like they own it." He ground a fist into one palm. "What they need is a lesson, y'know. And I didn't go through hell for this country just to be made a damned fool of."

"Now wait a minute, Harv," Patrick said, half rising from his chair, his heart pounding, blood swirling. "Don't be an idiot. Good god, man, you're damned near my age!"

Harv leaned back slowly, drawing himself up to his full height. "Damned near— What the hell are you trying to say, Pat? That I can't take care of myself anymore?"

"For crying out loud, Harvey, I didn't mean that at all." But the words as he spoke them lacked any conviction.

"Yeah," the janitor said. He looked to Karen, who looked away; to Jack, who had left his corner and was smirking by the window; to Pat, whose gaze searched the office for a clue to reason. "Yeah, I'm an old man who talks too much about the good old days, right? Put my money where my mouth is, right? Ain't that what you're saying, Pat? Put my money where my mouth is?" He lifted a fist made smaller and uglier by the loss of three fingers. "Never knew you thought so little of me, Patrick. You and your stupid goddamn trombone."

"No!" he said; but Harv was already out the door and moving across the lobby. With a strangled appeal for support he rushed around the desk and followed the big man to the front door. He was too late. Harv was already standing outside on the top step, hands on his hips, one foot tapping the concrete impatiently.

Patrick moved to join him, but the door would not open.

Tony's body still lay there, its dead hand beseeching.

Harv grabbed the center railing and pulled himself down as though moving through a gel, avoided Tony's body and headed for the riders. Suddenly he doubled over, and Patrick's hand went to his stomach in sympathetic pain. But the janitor straightened painfully and took a second step, a third, before he was struck again.

His head twisted slowly from side to side, his chin out-thrust, his shoulders rolling. Another pace, angling now away from the motionless leader toward the rider immediately to his left. Patrick felt himself leaning forward, his hands to the near panes, willing Harvey strength while railing silently at the bikers.

It almost seemed then as if the man felt the connection. His head snapped away from an invisible blow, but his left hand reached out and grabbed the biker's wrist. The Harley wavered (it *moves!* Patrick thought triumphantly), the janitor struggled, and before Patrick could utter the cheer forming in his throat Harv had wrenched the black figure out of its seat.

It struggled, then (dear god, it *moves! it moves!*), and thrashed wildly in Harv's grip, legs trying to reach stomach and groin, hands reaching out for eyes and mouth.

Patrick heard Karen whimpering; she was watching after all.

The other riders seemed to stir. It was little more than a shimmering of concentrated blackness, but the source-less light appeared less distinct, less threatening. He was sure he saw a head move in Harv's direction, wasn't quite as sure he saw a hand flexing in a glove.

The figure was down on its knees, its face pressed hard into the janitor's abdomen, its arms limp at its sides, it legs no longer kicking. Its cap had fallen into the gutter.

"Yes," Patrick whispered, almost jumping in place. "Yes, yes!"

With a sudden, disdainful shove, Harv tossed the rider into the street, and the bike toppled over onto its thighs. There was no cry, no crash, just a slow tumbling and a raising of dust. Then he moved to the next one, good hand out and ready to grab.

"Yes," Patrick whispered, louder than before.

Harv stopped, frozen, and Patrick sensed some confusion.

"Do it, you idiot," he said, and kicked at the unmoving door frantically. "Damnit, Harv!"

The outstretched arm dropped slowly, and Harv sagged to his knees on the curb. He shook his head as though trying to clear it, put his hands to his ears and lowered them again, stared at them . . . and turned.

In the office, Karen screamed.

Patrick fell against the door when his knees buckled, his cheek pressed to a pane, one eye opened and staring.

Harv's face was gone. Flesh, muscle, cartilage had vanished, the skull gleaming brightly as if it had just been washed. The hands too had been stripped, and his clothes hung on his frame loosely, rippling in the breeze that stirred Tony's hair.

Patrick could not look away.

He could not avoid the gradual collapse of his friend, nor the sensation more than the sound of the skull striking concrete.

And he could not help hearing the silent scream of the man's eyes still wide in their sockets.

12:05 A.M.

He leaned over the basin and doused his face, his head with sharply cold water. He sputtered and splashed himself again, half hoping some of the water would find its way into his lungs and drown him as he stood there. He had thought about dying before, when he had gripped the sides of the toilet bowl and emptied his stomach, when he'd wept as the acid boiled into his mouth and between his lips, when it was done but his stomach refused to cease its tireless convulsions—when he had lurched to his feet and saw his face in the mirror, the face of an old man whose hair had matted over his forehead to somehow and perversely give the impression of age falling away. He had been too tired to glare at it, or wonder at it; all he could do was stare at it and question the sanity that persisted in those eyes. He took to the water again, not caring that it was staining his trousers, darkening his shoes, puddling on the floor and making it slippery; anything, even the simplest of displeasures, was better than seeing Harv being murdered again, or rushing into the office once he could use his legs to find Karen slumped in the far corner while Jack stood at the window and watched the riders. He knew he had shouted something, but he couldn't remember what it had been; he had shouted, and he had run from the room, careening toward the back and toppling sacks and warrens and tables and chairs without feeling a thing. Now there was an aching where his thighs had taken their beating, where his fingers had gripped and had been stripped away, where his lungs had expelled the air and sucked in fire. And the water wasn't doing him a damned bit of good, though at the moment he could not think of anything else to do.

Finally, he stopped and took hold of the basin's slick sides. He lowerd his head and spat, spat again and reached blindly for the paper towels. They were rough on his face, and he scrubbed harder, slowing only when he began to fear he would draw blood from the pink surface. Not that it mattered. Bleed now, bleed later,

what was the difference when those . . . those things
out there were going to kill him anyway. Sooner or
later. And the customers would come to the post office
in the morning and find Tony's head in the gutter and
Harv's skeleton beside it and whatever was going to
happen to him here in the building. It would be hell on
the day's deliveries. Assuming Jack and Karen were
going to die, too, and why not. What was so special
about them that they would be spared. The only question was in the method of the dying. And no matter how
it happened there would be an investigation and a report and a solemn mass funeral in the Memorial Park and
his life would be relegated to hushed stories by the fireplace, in the bars, in the luncheonette and the Inn; and
people would say, please, not while I'm eating, and the
tellers would grin and go into more detail, all the while
protesting they were only giving the facts.

An investigation. A report. A ghost story by the
hearth.

He brushed an errant drop off the end of his nose and
checked his reflection again.

Then, abruptly, he spun away and stalked out of the
restroom. He had seen something in that fool mirror;
something that should not have been there. In the eyes.
In those large brown eyes that would not flinch as he
watched them.

Back in the office he paid no attention to Jack, nor
did he give more than a perfunctory glance to the scene
outside the window. Instead, he knelt beside Karen and
put a hand lightly on her shoulder. She was lying on her
side facing the wall, her knees drawn up toward her
chest, her hands clasped under her chin. He had the
feeling that it would not be long before she was sucking

her thumb. He shook her gently, but she did not open her eyes. Harder, and her head lolled on the floor. Quickly, he placed a hand over her heart—a slight twinge of guilt as he felt the bulge of her breast—and waited without breathing until he could detect the steady thump of her heart.

He exhaled his relief loudly and rocked back on his heels, concern for her welfare abruptly replaced by a swift, short-lived surge of anger. She was supposed to have been one of the strongest among them: she had raised three children alone, had set them on their way to college, had endured slanders and snickers and had maintained her integrity. Now she was retreating into a world where neither he nor Jack was welcome. Missy, he thought incongruously, would have disapproved. Missy, who was taller than her mother and full-breasted and determined that no one short of God was going to bring hell to her life. Missy, who, when he saw her, made him wish he were twenty years younger and ten times more virile. The slope of her pale throat, the push of her blouses, the flare of her hips, the way she walked along the pavement as though the world were her court and she the Virgin Queen.

Damn!

He stood quickly and wiped his hands on his trousers. What was he doing, thinking like that when there was draped around his shoulders a chilled cloak of fear.

He blinked rapidly. Swallowed. Supposed that his mind was trying to find an outlet for that very same fear, working to concentrate on anything but the tightening of his skin across his shoulders and the loosening of his bowels and the certain knowledge that this was one adventure he was not going to escape simply by turning away, or telling himself he was not the type to indulge in such fancies.

Fear made some men cowards and other men angry, and here he was thinking of a tryst with Melissa Redmond. A child. But when he looked back to Karen he couldn't help but feel angry.

1:50 A.M.

The silence was beginning to shred at his nerves. He had tried to get Jack to talk to him several times, but Fawn would only grunt and stare out the window. Karen was stirring, but she would not respond when he shook her, nudged her hard with his toe, once slapped at her shoulder harder than was necessary. So he walked out of the office and began stalking the back room, slamming down books of regulations, throwing letters and packages, just to hear them pass through the air.

Several times he considered methods of escape.

First he attacked the rear door with the metal chair to his metal desk. When the back crumpled and one leg dislodged, he tossed it aside contemptuously, hurried after it and kicked it all the way to the front, stopping only when he could no longer catch his breath without feeling dizzy.

Then he gathered as much mail as he could and heaped it in a pile against the plaster wall. As he dug into his pockets for a match he found his holder and jammed it into his mouth. Chewed on it furiously. Found the match and lighted it and held it near the paper. When the flame reached his thumb he dropped it with a start and stared at the black cardboard that had once been a match. No fire, he decided. Before it worked its way through the wall or ceiling he would have suffocated because, he felt, none of the smoke would escape through the windows he would have broken in front. Assuming, of course, he could have broken them in the first place.

Finally, refusing to give way to the swell of frustration that was building in his chest, he ransacked the small storeroom for Harv's tools and methodically broke them all as he tried to pry open the rear door, the restroom window, dig through the plaster to the outside brick.

He lifted the heaviest mail sack he could find and tossed it almost effortlessly through the frosted glass, grinning when he heard the crystal tinkling on the marble floor. He threw another one. Another. Continued to lift and throw until there was nothing left but the spiraled bars of the cages thin-framed in oak. Then he walked through the office to the front door and stared at the riders.

2:40 A.M.

The first biker on the left moved. It half rose and kicked down. The Harley sputtered and caught, and the grumbling was lulling in the quiet hours of the morning.

2:45 A.M.

The first biker on the right moved. It half rose and kicked down. The Harley sputtered and caught, and the grumbling was soothing in the quiet hours of the morning.

2:50 A.M.

The three inside bikers moved. They half rose and kicked down. Their Harleys sputtered and caught, and the grumbling was beckoning in the quiet hours of the morning.

3:30 A.M.

Patrick finally wrenched away from the door and hurried into the office. He could not stand there waiting for the leader to start his machine too, could not bring himself to watch the faint plumes of exhaust lift into the air and hang there like fog. It was maddening, as he was sure it was meant to be, and he was not about to surrender to their madness now, not after waiting for so many hours for something to happen. At first there had been hope that they'd tire of the game, and at first he could not believe that he was listening to those engines. He'd thought they'd finally broken him until he'd heard Jack grunting as if urging them on, away, out of the night to let the dawn come unsullied. Then he had found patience to watch them and listen, until the watching and the listening became a weight on his shoulders and a band around his throat.

He moved to the desk and switched off the lamp. The soft, weak glow was transformed into a greylight that curiously managed to rid the room of its shadows. He looked to the window. Jack was gone, and before he could search he heard Karen stirring. Remembering the anger he had felt and the kicks at her side, he almost broke into an apology as she lifted herself by stages to sit against the wall.

"Are they . . ." She stopped, listened, and shook her

head slowly. "It was a nice idea," she said.

"What was," he said, sitting down beside her.

"The dream. All that talk about me dreaming. It was a nice idea for a while, wasn't it."

"Yeah," he said, pulling the holder from his mouth and looking at it distastefully. He tossed it away, saw it bounce against the doorjamb and spin into the lobby, over the broken glass that glittered like lost stars. "Yeah, it was a nice idea, Karen. I wish to hell it was the answer."

"Have you figured it out yet?"

He shook his head.

She brushed at her shirt, and his gaze could not help lingering at the swell of her breasts, the shadows that writhed there as she respositioned herself. When he was drawn to her face he saw she'd been watching. Caught, then, he did not look away; it would only make it worse.

"I heard noises," she said.

He explained what he had been doing over the past two or three hours, almost laughing at the sight of himself rampaging through the mail. And when he felt the grin on his face he held it, glad for any small thing that would temporarily mask his fear.

Fear, he thought, and rubbed his arms briskly. It occurred to him then that he was not at all afraid. Not any longer. And that, in itself, was frightening enough.

"I've decided," she said quietly, without looking directly at him but rather in a sidelong gaze that also caught the front door, "that I'm going to die."

"Don't be stupid," he said automatically. Then, with conviction: "Don't be stupid, Karen! As long as we stay in here we're not going to die."

"But how do we know they won't come in after us?"

"Because they would have done it long before this, right?"

"How do you know?" she pressed. "How do you know that for sure?"

He said nothing. He wondered where Jack had gone to, wondered suddenly if that slimy black-haired punk had found a way out and had taken it without telling his friends. Gratitude for you, damnit, he thought. There I was, breaking every regulation in the book and setting myself up for all kinds of charges and the sonofabitch lights out without showing me the way. Us, he corrected quickly; without showing us the way.

He shifted his buttocks, and heard Karen moving slightly away from him. He looked over and stared, and saw the veil over her eyes.

"What's the matter?" he said. "You . . . are you all right?"

"It just occurred to me," she said, struggling to her feet to put the desk between them. "It just occurred to me that you killed them, Pat."

His mouth opened, closed; he looked to the doorway, to the window, to the ceiling. "What?"

"You did!"

A hand to his forehead, to his mouth, to his cheek. "Karen, I don't understand what you're talking about." He wanted to cry. She had returned to the Station with her mind broken by fear and scrambled by terror. He grunted and smiled. He almost said *you're crazy*. "You don't know what you're saying. How could I kill them, huh? I was here all the time."

She shook her head, confused. "I don't know. But it came to me while I was . . . while I was away. You had a part in it, Pat. You're one of them, aren't you."

He could not contain the disgust that he felt. "For god's sake, Karen!"

"But damnit, Pat, you enjoyed it! I saw you! You egged Tony and Harv on until they had to go out there and face them down. You forced them out there, and then you enjoyed watching them die. I *saw* you, Pat. I saw the look on your face."

The head snapped back . . . back . . . tearing loose from the neck and rolling to the curb; the flesh fell away to expose the bone and the eyes in the sockets were trapped and screaming.

"Look at you, damnit! You're actually grinning!"

He swallowed, and lifted a hand in protest. But Karen let out a choked cry and bolted from the room. Into the lobby. Across the splinters and islands and icebergs of glass that slipped under her feet and tripped her. By the time he reached the threshold she had slid over the marble and had plunged through the door headfirst, her screams lifting to the vaulted ceiling and clinging there like burrs. He stared at the nearest caged window, listening to her screams; he clawed his hands into fists, and listened to her screams; he searched the dim back room for Jack . . . and listened to her screams.

And he knew that as long as he refused to walk to the door and look out at the street she would lie there on the broad stoop and scream forever.

He wanted to vomit, and remembered the look in his eyes after Harvey had died.

He called out for Jack, and thought he saw movement back by the restroom.

He jumped back into the office and sat at his desk, staring at Washington and covering his ears.

3:50 A.M.

Screaming.

4:00 A.M.

Screaming.

4:30 A.M.

Screaming.

5:00 A.M.

NO!''
He pounded at the desk until his hands were bloddied and the sight of the red brought knives to his eyes. They worked at the lids to keep them open, worked at the edges until he wept.

5:10 A.M.

NO! NO! Goddamnit, *NO!*''

5:15 A.M.

He stood suddenly and kicked back the chair, shoved at the desk until it slid over against the wall. The way was clear to the lobby, and he took it. Stumbling over shadows. His stomach churning bile that would not rise to his mouth. His hands flapping uselessly at his sides, his elbows crooked and his neck at an odd angle. His tongue flicked at the air, at his lips, and saliva slipped from the taut corner of his mouth to slide to his chin and gleam there unmoving. His hair was streaked with thin bands of dark brown; his cheeks had lost their hollowed depression.

He kicked aside the shards of frosted glass.

He saw that the doors were still slightly ajar.

The head. . . and the bone.

Karen's left foot was keeping the doors open, and he could see through the narrow slit that she had torn off her nails clawing at the concrete while reaching for the iron railing that Harvey had grabbed. Her hair was matted with perspiration and blood, the backs of her hands stripped raw to the muscle.

Her mouth was wide open, and he could still hear her screaming. Screaming while the engines still thrummed invitation.

"Don't."

He had reached down to grab for her shoe, to pull her in so she could see she was wrong.

The warning came again: "Don't touch it, Pat. Please don't touch it."

He straightened involuntarily and turned. Jack had climbed to the top of what was left of the partition and was standing above him, hands in his pockets, his face cadaverous and saddened. Patrick gestured to the doors helplessly, and when his mouth groped for words he could feel the dried tears that had caked on his cheeks.

Suddenly, he felt old.

Jack leapt to the floor and landed without a sound, leaned against the remains of the wall and folded his arms over his chest. "Just leave it be, Pat. It'll be over by dawn."

They both looked to the round-faced clock on the wall over the door. An hour at most of listening to her screaming.

"I can't."

Jack shrugged. "You have to."

"I don't want her to die."

"She will whether you bring her in here or not. Sooner or later." He grinned.

Patrick bridled. "What the hell is it with you, anyway? How can you laugh when something like this is happening? What are you, some kind of monster? Are you one of them, Jack? Are you their . . . do you scout towns for them, victims, show them who to kill and who to keep alive?" He took a step forward, suddenly filled with righteous self-hatred. "Well? Answer me, youngster! What do I have to do, drive a stake through your heart?"

"Which one do you want me to answer," Jack said pleasantly.

Patrick narrowed his eyes and took another step. "All of them," he said, his voice low and warning.

"Well . . . no, you don't have to drive a stake through my heart. Or shoot me with silver bullets. Or say the magic word so I'll disappear in a flare of sulphur and fire. No, Pat, I'm not the Devil or anything like him."

"But you are one of them," he said, insisting now because it was finally the time to know.

Jack hesitated and took out his comb. Patrick glared at it, took one final step and slapped it away. It scuttled over the floor and lodged against the baseboard; and for the first time he noted that Fawn seemed more than uneasy, more than discomforted.

"Well?" His voice was stronger. Now it demanded.

And still Karen screamed.

Jack lowered his arms to his sides slowly, almost as if it pained him to do it. The pockmarks on his face had taken on shadows that added a darkness to his years that had not been there that morning, and his eyes had lost their perpetual sardonic glitter.

"I'm not one of them," he said, so softly Patrick had to lean closer to hear him. "But I used to be. For a long time, Pat, and I saw a lot of the country, saw a lot of people from San Francisco to New York and every damned place in between." He stirred, and his voice took the hint of melancholy pride. "In fact, as long as you're asking, I used to ride that lead bike once in a while. It was damned nice, riding into a town ahead of the others, watching for the faces you would know when you saw them."

"What do you mean by that?"

Jack ignored him. "The trouble was, like all the rest of them sooner or later, I wanted something more. Oh, it was fun—"

"Fun?"

"—figuring out ways to do things to people. One time I remember putting a whole office building under. One at a time. Damn, but the night lasted long that day! One at a time, and every one of them different. I'll tell you one thing, Pat: it took a lot of imagination."

Patrick gestured at him in revulsion and disgust. "I don't know what you're talking about. Is this some kind of drug you're talking about? How can you hold a whole office building without someone getting out?" But he turned away without waiting for an answer.

Karen . . . screaming.

Of course it could be done, he told himself as if he were lecturing to a stupid child. If they can keep five of us penned in here like sheep to the slaughter, why not fifty? Why not five hundred? Because, he thought as that last figure flashed, there had to be a limit to what they could do or they would take hold of a country and not bother with a village.

But it stll did not answer all of his questions, nor did

it tell him why Karen had said all those horrid things to him. Certainly he had been watching when the other two had died; he had been right there, hadn't he? And he knew he wasn't any better or any worse than anyone else in the world, that just like all of them he would slow down when he passed an accident, would stop when he saw a jumper on a ledge . . . but he never urged the jumping nor thirsted after the blood—that was merely a symptom of the Roman circus mentality.

No. At least he could say he never thirsted after the blood.

And suddenly the evening telescoped to a sentence. He looked at Jack, who was looking at the doors. "You said something earlier. You said they used to be horses."

Jack nodded again.

Patrick grunted as Karen kept screaming, and he walked into the office to stare at the dead phone. Returned to the lobby to stare at the man.

"It's no joke," Jack said.

"Then how *old* are you?" He had wanted it to be a command; it had come out the whisper of a frightened old man.

"Old enough to want out," Jack said, refolding his arms. "The trouble is, you don't get out."

"Out. Out. Get out from what?" He whirled to the door. "And why the hell doesn't she stop that goddamned screaming?"

"She will," Jack said. "She will."

Patrick's mouth dried, and swallowing was like forcing down straw.

"Out from them," Jack told him, lifting his chin in a sweep toward the front. Then he turned to him and smiled. "It's the excitement, you see. Like running away to join the circus, only this time you run away to join . . .them. Thrills, adventure, the scent of the hunt and the close for the kill. Not everybody can do it, you know. There has to be something dead inside you, something that turns off the tears when you see someone you love die, or when a child is murdered, or when . . . well, you get the picture, Pat. Someone like me."

"I don't believe it."

"Yes you do, Pat. You believe it because you felt it a little a couple of times tonight. Karen was right. You'd better admit it, old man: you couldn't help feeling just a little excited when you saw what they could do, when you saw what they did."

There were tears of shame that welled but would not run.

"But you get tired of it after a while. I've been with them for . . . let's say years, all right? A lot of years, old man. I started young, before I was fifteen, and that's a lot of years to grow older so slowly. I got tired, and I got out . . . and those damned riders found me."

Patrick could not help but ask: "To do what?"

Jack shrugged. "Get me back or kill me."

"Why? Because you'd tell?" His laugh was bitter. "Who would believe you?"

"You do."

"I'm in here. Out there in broad daylight, why they'd laugh you right into the funny farm, Jack. You know that."

"I know a lot of other things, too."

Patrick nodded. "Yes, I suppose you do."

Karen . . .

"Are you . . . are you going back?"

"I don't know. I haven't made up my mind. There has to be eight, you know. That's why Harv was able to get as close as he did. But they stopped him. Now they're missing two, and they'll have to find someone else."

"It must be hard."

Jack grinned, and his teeth took the greylight and made it shine. "Not that hard, old man. You don't always know what you're getting into. And once you're into it . . . well, sometimes it can be fun."

The bile in his stomach lurched again, and he pressed a hand to his belt to calm it until it subsided. "What," he asked then, "if you don't come out by dawn? Will they come in after you?"

"When everyone's dead, yes."

Patrick sagged against the wall, his palms spread beside him to keep him from falling. He had asked one question and had received the answer to the one he couldn't form. Then, suddenly, he could no longer stand the death screams of the woman and he bolted for the door as Jack shouted at him hysterically. He grabbed the shoe and began pulling, tugging hard until he realized the doors were wedged and he would have to open one wider. He reached out and pushed, and the shoe slipped from his hand.

Karen screamed once, and was silent.

Patrick dropped to his knees and saw her slip over the stoop to the steps, slide down them to the sidewalk. A dark red stain was left behind her. When she reached the leader he lifted his bootheel over her head. And held it while Karen twisted around to catch the plea in Patrick's eyes.

Jack bellowed incoherently and slammed through the other door.

The boot came down.

Patrick heard the skull crack loudly.

Then he scrambled to his feet just as Fawn lunged for the nearest rider, toppling it from its seat and grappling with it on the roadway. He stepped outside without realizing it, became suddenly aware of his position and turned around to reenter. Paused. Looked back over his shoulder at the gleam of the chrome and the promise of the black.

He tried then to remember everything he'd been taught.

"Pat, help me!"

Sundays in church and extolling the Golden Rule. Muttering an "excuse me" whenever a young kid bumped into him without thinking. Giving advice to Karen whenever her life fell apart, which seemed to happen with monotonous regularity. The Ten Commandments that were obeyed whenever it was convenient for the preacher and the congregation. The loopholes, like tax laws, that allowed permissive coupling and venality and war.

"Pat . . . help me. I don't . . ."

What would it be like, he wondered, to ride into a town and hold people hostage. Hold them, knowing that sooner or later they would run into your arms so you could do what you liked. It was kind of interesting, actually. It would be like an experiment. How much pain could you inflict, how much torture could a man take, how long could you keep it up until, like Jack, it all paled and lost its meaning.

He watched as Jack was thrown onto the sidewalk, his

head meeting the pavement with a thud that stunned him.

Tony's head; Harvey's bone; Karen's blood.

He had to admit it wouldn't lack excitement, and excitement was something he had avoided all his life.

No. It didn't make any difference how young he felt, nor how intellectually curious he was, nor how tempting it was to live out his life on a wave of electric fervor. Argue both sides, and it still came out . . . wrong. It was as simple as that; riding with these creatures, with these modern dragons and the night would be pure and simple evil. And when he thought of all the people— men, women, and children—who had died at their hands he felt the anger rekindling, felt the ember fan to flame.

It was exciting, but it was wrong; it was wrong, but it was exciting.

His eyes closed briefly, opened, and he rushed down the steps and knelt at Jack's side. He could feel the riders watching as he swept a hand through the black hair streaked now with grey. Jack was still alive, a pulse throbbing below his temple, and Patrick glared up at the leader as he waited for his friend to waken. Looked higher and saw the sky beginning to lighten.

They could have killed him, he thought then; they could have killed him where he knelt, but they no longer had the power.

He smiled.

The bikers were restless; he could see their machines trembling.

"Bastards," he said to them as loudly as he could, as hard as he dared.

Thunder/noise, growing.

His smile broadened to a grin. "Can't do it alone, right? You can't even kill a helpless old man." He laughed, and the dark hours after sunset drained in the sound.

Concerts in the park, sorting mail and joking, walking the streets to the door of his home.

Autumn. The perfect season.

Jack groaned, and Patrick looked down to him, laughed and put his hands around his throat.

Autumn. The perfect season.

Endlessly dying.

PART IV

Winter, 1970

THE COLOR
OF JOY

It was the holiday season, by calendar and by spirit, and the small house on Quentin Avenue observed tradition faithfully, up to and including the party given on the Friday before Christmas itself.

On the front door was a wreath. A real one. With a great red bow in its center and tiny silver globes buried in the branches that wound about the wire frame. The nearest streetlamp just managed to strain under the porch roof and touch it, so that the bow and the globes seemed brighter than they were, and clearer, and purer.

In the tiny foyer, crowded now with coats and hats and a few cashmere scarves precariously clinging to the coatracks against either wall, an equally tiny chandelier with teardrop bulbs was touched by a sprig of mistletoe. A real one. With a small red bow and tiny white berries and gleaming green leaves that pricked when you grabbed them.

The Christmas tree, set up a full week before the holiday and just in time for the party, stood in the front room's wide bow window, bedecked and lighted and filling the house with the pungent scent of dying pine. Beneath its lowest boughs packages were scattered, almost all of them hollow despite the ribbons and the seasonal paper and the light dusting of needles. No one touched them. Few gave them more than a polite, cursory glance. The guests knew they were artifice and knew their purpose and only one or two, quite late in the evening, bothered to kneel by the tree and give some of them a tentative, almost embarrassed shake.

The room to the right of the foyer held the long walnut table that had taken an hour to polish, two hours to cover with bowls and trays, silverware and glasses, a pair of pewter candelabra whose tallows were tall, red and unnervingly slender. There was no place to sit down here, all the chairs had been taken into the living room and the study, but people stayed anyway, either near the food or near the butler's table laden with bottles most of whose seals had been broken.

The study behind the living room was just that: bookshelves, a captain's desk, several weathered and comfortable armchairs, a faded globe on a brass stand, hunting prints on the paneled walls, and a curtained rear window that overlooked a small back yard. The light here was dim, the smoke heavy in spite of the fact that the window was open top and bottom, and more than a few careless spills had stained the burgundy carpet near the entrance to the narrow hallway across from which was the kitchen.

Upstairs: two bedrooms, a bath, two rooms in the back unused but cleaned.

At the head of the stairs was a round window over a window seat filled with stuffed toys and old games whose pieces had long since slipped under chairs and under beds and behind doors . . . and disappeared.

Melissa Redmond stood at the window and looked down at the yard. There were ghosts there, shaded by the cherry trees and frightened by the soft noise that slipped out of the house and over the dead grass. She saw them clearly, and as she watched she brought her glass to one cheek and held it there. For the cold that penetrated, and for the reminder that the ghosts were too long in their fading.

A young man in a tweed three-piece suit came up the carpeted steps to join her, not touching and not speaking but breathing deliberately loudly so he would not startle her when she turned. He waited for almost five minutes.

"You have people downstairs, Mel," he said. Behind dark-rimmed glasses his eyes were large and brown, and he blinked them rapidly while one hand reached absently to flatten a cowlick that sprouted at the back of his head.

"I know," she said, though not at all contrite, and not at all sadly. "But sometimes . . . I come up here sometimes, Mike, and I can still see them all down there. Eddie and Stan working in the garden, Mother standing beside them with her hands on her hips and giving them orders. Eddie wouldn't pay any attention to her, and Stan would laugh to make her mad." She sipped from the glass; it was filled with ginger ale. "She put up with a lot from us, you know."

Michael nodded, though Mel knew he had never met her mother. "It's the season," he told her solemnly.

Melissa turned and looked up at him, grinning. "Am I supposed to take comfort from that, Counselor?" When he frowned, she touched his arm and stroked it. "Relax, I'm not going to jump out, if that's what you're worried about."

"I just want you to be happy, that's all."

"So who isn't?"

She moved around him to look down the stairwell.

Several people wandered past, through the foyer to the living room, and from the study she could hear the giggling strains of an abortive carol.

"I just don't like the idea of you being alone in here," he told her.

She frowned, but would not let him see it. "Mike, I'm a big girl, or hadn't you noticed? I'm nearly thirty. I have a good job, and my love life is . . . well, let's just say it's reasonably satisfactory."

"I still don't like the idea of you being alone."

She would have turned on him, then, and told him she didn't give a damn what he thought, that she was tired of him dogging her every minute of the day just because he believed her to be some sort of helpless female caught in the throes of the suicide season. But her attention was diverted by a couple heading up toward her. The man was extraordinarily tall, lean, bald without apology and sporting a handlebar mustache waxed into comic curls at either end; the woman was Melissa's age, much stouter (though definitely not fat), and wearing a tight black sheath that barely allowed her legs to move; as it was, she had to pull up its skirt to permit her to take the stairs without moving sideways.

"You," the man said, pointing at her with a finger manicured and tanned, "are supposed to be down there hostessing, or whatever the hell."

"And you," she told him, "are supposed to be down there guesting, or whatever."

He rolled his eyes and sighed loudly. "Samuel Thompson Litten is trying to remember the original words to 'Greensleeves,' and I'd sooner die than have to sit there and wait for him to give it up."

The landing was somewhat crowded now, but Mel

didn't make a move toward any of the rooms. She liked it here, in the center of the house, and brushed Mike politely to one side to take part of the window seat. The woman immediately sat beside her.

"Mel," she said, throaty, slightly slurred, "this is the best party you've ever given."

"It's the first one, Tammy," she said, almost losing her grip on a laugh.

"I know. You shouldn't give another. You'll spoil your record."

Mel looked to Mike, who shrugged, and to Paul, who only stared at his shoes.

There was a silence, a long one, before Tammy cleared her throat.

"Mel, Paul and I want you to come to our place for Christmas breakfast." She said it in a rush, as if she'd been wanting to get it out all night and hadn't had the nerve. And when she was done, a faint blush rose from her neck to spill onto her cheeks. It complemented her black hair perfectly, made brighter her black eyes. "Really," she said then. "Really."

"Oh, I believe you," Mel said quickly, a hand to Tammy's leg. "And that is about the best Christmas present either of you could have given me."

"Told you she wouldn't come," Paul said, though Mel could sense he wasn't entirely displeased.

"She didn't say that," his wife protested.

"Yes I did," Mel told her. "You just weren't listening."

Tammy hiccoughed, covered her mouth and blushed even harder. "Am I drunk?"

"No," Paul said.

"Not yet," Mike said.

"Yes I am. Oh damn, why do I do this? Every time we go out I think I've figured it out right. One before dinner, one during snacks, two while I try to keep Paul from grabbing at every butt in a dress." She shook her head slowly. "Somehow I always manage to lose track."

"After the first one," Paul said, and skipped backward to avoid the swing of her pointed shoe. "Shame, woman, you'll make a spectacle of yourself. Michael, do I have grounds for suit here? For that matter, can I sue my own wife?"

"Well," Mike said, a hand to his chin, the other in his jacket pocket, "I'll have to take that under advisement, if you don't mind. There's precedent to be searched out, of course, not to mention the financial status of the defendant." He grinned at Tammy, who was looking bewildered. "That's you, Tam."

Paul then questioned—at the top of his basso voice—Mike's credentials, and Mel snuggled back into the corner to listen to the banter. It was not particularly original, nor was it especially humorous, but it belonged to her friends and was for that reason extraordinarily special. And in thinking how special they all were to her, she decided that she was, in fact, one of the most lucky people she had ever known. And the happiest. Not that everything was absolutely perfect: the house wanted painting first thing in the spring, her boss at the college seemed more interested in her bust than in her paperwork, and her car was beginning to act its age; but all in all there was nothing wrong with her life. Not now. Not anymore.

She was even loved by the three people standing around her, and several more waiting for her downstairs; what more could she want, then?

It certainly wasn't like the first day she had returned to the Station.

"Mel?"

She had come in on the bus, brave, determined, chin set and heart calmed. And it would have been all right if the vehicle hadn't stopped at the corner of the Pike and Centre Street, if it hadn't shuddered for nearly a full minute waiting for traffic and forcing her to look down at the doors to the post office. At the place where the bodies had been found. At the curb where her mother had been discovered at dawn, her heart stopped, her clothing torn, but otherwise untouched. The blame had been set—if not legally, at least popularly—on the missing postmaster, but she hadn't cared about that. It wasn't the point. The point was, her mother was dead and she had been left to see to it that her brothers were raised the way it had all been planned from the day her father had taken off for god knew where. And she had done it. With more help than she could have imagined was possible from the church and her neighbors she had managed to graduate from high school, get a job and wait for Eddie and Stan to do the same. Then, with the insurance money and savings, she had gone off to college for the education her mother had demanded, in life as well as in dreams after death.

Her brothers, however, had weathered a furious battle around the kitchen table one night and had both joined the Army. They had convinced her it was cheaper, better for them, better for her, and they probably would have been drafted anyway, so what was the difference?

The difference was, they never came back. Eddie died

in a plane crash on his way from Basic to Advanced Training; and Stan was brought back from Saigon in a flag-draped coffin—and that was before anyone even knew there was a war.

"Mel, are you listening to me?"

She had stayed away, then. The house was rented, and the money was used to send her through graduate school to supplement the scholarships. Used to send her around the world. Used to bring her back when she discovered that her mother and brothers were dead, gone, never to return, and there was no sense searching every damned street in every damned country because they would never show up again and as soon as she realized it the sooner she would see that she was killing herself with dreams and delusions and quiet night-weeping.

And it would have been profit if the bus hadn't stopped in front of the post office and she'd been forced to remember—too soon, too soon—the manner of the dying.

But that had been the first day. The second was somewhat better. The third better still. And on the fourth she landed the position at the community college and within two weeks school had begun and so had her living.

A hand gripped her shoulder and shook it gently. She watched the bus fade, the post office fade, the reflection of herself in that dust-streaked window shimmer into that of a dark-haired woman with large black eyes and gleaming red lips and dimples in both cheeks that almost made her pretty.

"Huh?"

Laughter cloaked her and made her grin sheepishly, brought her up from the window seat with a playful slap at each of them. Someone called to her from below and she shrugged elaborately before heading downstairs, where she was swept almost instantly into the middle of an argument that began, centered around and finally ended an hour later with indictments drunk and sober against the person of the President. Mel tried to follow them as carefully as she could, tried to comment when called upon for arbitration, but thought it all too much like spearing fish in a teacup. Straw men and hot air. Especially when someone attempted a comparison between the Nixon Administration and the events portrayed in Z; that was too much, and she excused herself, laughing, poked her head into the study, where Sam Litten was struggling with notes never meant for his throat, and left again, this time heading for the front porch and what she hoped was a breath of somewhat fresh air.

It was cold and dry outside, the bare trees and spikes of grass appearing as through a pane of not-quite-clear glass—sharp-edged and brittle and waiting for the snow. A few houses across the street were already dark, and those still lighted seemed remarkably distant. She hugged herself against the cold, then moved a hand up to draw lightly at her throat.

A car sped past left to right, heading out toward the valley. At the intersection with Park Street only two houses over she could see a small animal stalking a shadow. A dead leaf dropped into the streetlight and froze for a moment, suspended on end, breaking for the gutter only when the door behind her opened and Sam Litten stepped out.

"Brother! They have no appreciation of fine music, Mel. None at all."

She smiled and set an elbow into his ribs. He was no

taller than she, but rotund and pink-faced and trying to salvage with considerable lack of success what brown there was left in what was left of his hair. His leather-patched jacket was tweed, his tie old school, his shirt white, his trousers just short enough to reveal socks that were falling down around his ankles.

He groaned, stretched, and turned to face her, and Mel closed her eyes briefly against the friendly assault of his gaze.

"Dr. Redmond, you're going to catch pneumonia, you know."

He started at the top, touching her quiet red hair parted in the center and falling near to her shoulders; moved to her face and the deep-set green eyes, the narrow stubbed nose, the freckle-sprayed cheeks, the round of her chin; to the chest she had once considered binding to make less prominent, to the prim waistline and the long, slender legs. When she felt he was done she opened her eyes and managed a smile.

He seemed flustered and looked away quickly, out to the street. "Awfully quiet for a Friday night," he said.

She nodded. "Must be the weather."

The sky had been overcast for several days, threatening snow but delivering nothing but pale ghosts of shadows and the blocking of the moon.

"I imagine you're pretty booked up for the holidays. New Year's and all that."

"I imagine I am," she said.

He shook his head sorrowfully. "Just my luck. Just my luck."

No, she thought, my luck.

He clapped his hands together and rubbed them vigorously. "Well, I expect I'll see you at the Department meeting on Monday."

"I expect you will."

He hunched his shoulders as though against the cold, turned and surprised her by placing a soft kiss on her cheek. "In case there's no chance later," he told her. "Have a good Christmas, Mel." And he was back inside before she could reply.

"Hell," she muttered. He was two decades older than she and trying desperately not to reach fifty without sampling some of the so-called Youth Revolution. His problem was in his manner: he had no idea when to be aggressive and when to back off, when to espouse a current cause and when to debunk it. As such he always seemed to her to be like a small boy just climbing out of the cellar—eyes blinking in confusion, hands out to grab at something for support, trying to figure out what had changed . . . and why. And for that reason she could not dislike him, didn't bother to scold him when he played at the rake. He was just so pitiably helpless she never had the heart to be angry.

The sound of shattering glass startled her, brought the cold back to her, and she had just reached for the doorknob when she saw him.

Standing just at the edge of the streetlamp's far reach.

At first she thought he was waiting to cross the street (though there was no traffic), or waiting for a ride (but there was no car idling near him); then she realized he was watching the house, watching her. His hands were plunged deep into the pockets of a long black raincoat with double rows of brass buttons. The wide collar was pulled high in back, a broad-brimmed black hat slouched low over his face. She could not make out his features, but she knew instantly he was looking at her.

There was an impulse to take a step toward him, an impulse to call out; both were stifled, however, when the door was yanked away from her hand and Michael demanded to know if she intended to stay out there for the rest of the night. She looked at him, looked back to the streetlamp . . . and the man in the black raincoat was no longer there.

"Are you all right, Mel?"

She nodded. "Yes. Sure. Get me a drink, okay?" Once in the foyer she closed the door without looking back, shrugging without moving, though just before midnight she caught herself parting the dining-room curtains and staring out at the street.

On Monday the cold was still sharp, but a break in the clouds had brought a breath of warm sunshine. The opportunity was too fine to pass up, and Mel decided there was nothing for it but that she would have to walk out to the campus. It was something she did as often as the weather allowed. There was too much to miss when she drove, from the shadings of light beneath the trees along the way to the very taste and smell of air she breathed. All of it was as wonderful a delight as being with her friends, moreso since she had come late (or so she thought) to the acceptance of her mortality. To permit an automobile, then, to rob her of a single leaf, a single singing bird, was tantamount to committing the most foul sort of suicide. Too much; there was much too much she dared not enjoy.

And too much of what she believed that had to be shared with others.

A little more than two miles separated the house on Quentin and the campus out on Chancellor Avenue. A part of that was the twice-larger-than-normal blocks she

had to walk before reaching the broad road that stretched toward the valley. She took them briskly, hands in
coat pockets, hair lightly protected by an emerald-green
scarf. Several automobiles passed her, a few with
drivers she knew; none of them, however, stopped. It
had taken almost the entire semester, but finally she had
been able to convince both her colleagues and the few
students who commuted from the village that she
actually preferred walking to riding. Now they merely
honked a greeting, yelled a comment (most of the time
carried off by the wind) or slowly shook their heads at
the eccentricities of professors.

She loved it.

Just as she loved the falling away of the houses, the
crowding of the woodland down to the shoulder. On her
left, across the road, the tall iron fence surrounding the
park gave way to stone walls and elaborate hedges that
marked the estates reaching out into the valley. She had
been in some of those homes on one or two occasions,
the latest being a small dinner party given by Oliver
Hawkstead, who was rumored ready to leave his entire
fortune to the college. She had no illusions why she had
been invited: brains and decoration, and the predictable
leers from a dying old man. Now that she thought about
it, she laughed; in a way it had probably been somewhat
demeaning for a woman of her abilities; but on the
other hand, she wasn't about to let some vague principle
stand in the way of improving her own lot as well as the
campus's.

A truck rumbled by, a station wagon, a van. She kept
to the far side of the shoulder and turned slightly away
to avoid the backwash of the passing vehicles.

And stopped.

The trees—mostly oak, elm, and birch—were sparse here, the ground covered with their leaves. About two hundred yards into the woods the first signs of an upward slope appeared, the lap of the hills that cut off the Station from the rest of Connecticut on three sides. The shrubs were bare, spindly, revealing greyed and decaying logs and half-fallen boles. In one such area a dark figure stood. Motionless. Partially screened by a stubbornly green laurel.

Mel had no doubt it was the same man in the same coat she had seen at the house Friday night; but while she had been merely curious then, now she was battling to be more annoyed than apprehensive.

A light breeze played with stray curls beneath her scarf and she swiped at them impatiently, blinked when her hand passed over her eyes and took a step back.

The figure was gone; in its place a lightning-blackened stump.

A car blared a warning and she spun around, a hand to her mouth, the other half-raised to flag it down. It was well past her, however, and she gnawed lightly at her lower lip. This wasn't like her at all. And it was obvious that, though she hadn't thought of the stranger since the night of the party, he had made some sort of impression on her. One she new she would much rather do without.

She walked more quickly, and the sun disappeared beneath the grey blanket overhead. The temperature dropped. The woodland thickened. By the time she reached the entrance to the campus the first, tentative snowflakes had begun to hide in the tall grass and melt blackly on her shoulders.

Was it a friend, she wondered as she hurried on to the

meeting, someone who thinks this makes a pretty fair gag? Or someone she didn't know, someone who needed to know where she lived, where she worked, how she managed to get from one place to another. It was, all of it, ridiculous in the extreme, but she could not dislodge the images once they had wormed their way in. The man beneath the streetlamp, the man in the woods . . . he followed her into the lab where Litten had already begun to explain the procedure for exams, sat just behind her and addled her thinking to the point where twice she had to ask the chairman to repeat the simplest of instructions. He frowned at her, as did the others, but none of them said anything until, just before noon, the meeting adjourned for lunch in the cafeteria. Afterward, there was to be a general faculty meeting, the last before the holidays, but Mel was already devising excuses to skip it if she could.

At the door, however, Litten caught her arm and eased her back inside. "Mel, you all right?"

Her smile was weak. "Sure."

"You weren't here today." The little man was concerned, his left hand fussing with an ascot at his collar. "You didn't have any trouble getting here, did you?"

"No," she said. "I walked, as usual."

"Someone try to pick you up?" He laughed, then. "You know what I mean. Not for a ride."

She shook her head. Shrugged. "It's nothing, Sam. I just thought . . . I thought there was someone in the trees, watching me, that's all. It turned out to be a dead stump, but it's like a tune you don't know the title of and you can't get it out of your head, you know what I mean?"

"I know, believe me. Though I really can't be persuaded that the music these days has any tune." He took her elbow and they walked down the corridor, falling in with other, just-ended meetings. "But why should that bother you so much?"

"How should I know? Just one of those things, I guess."

"Just one of those wonderful things," he sang, dreadfully off key.

"Terrible," she said, shaking her head and laughing. "That's really god-awful."

"You biology people are damned snobs," he told her.

"Maybe, but you chemistry fools can't sing worth a damn."

He pouted, scuffed a foot, and she broke into a laugh that she knew was too long and too loud, leaning into him for a moment as if he were Michael and resting her cheek briefly against his arm. "I'm okay," she insisted. "It's the end of term, if you know what I mean. I'd probably get hysterical over anything at all."

"You really want me to believe that?"

She laughed again. "Boss, you can believe any damn thing you want to."

And the moment she heard herself say it, she regretted it. Litten was too anxious to be more than just a friend, and the look in his eyes told her he had taken the comment as a delicate, but definite, invitation to dance. And she wasn't thinking clearly enough to say anything to discourage him. As it was, then, he commandeered chairs and a table for them in the cafeteria, made sure they were sitting together to listen to the dean of faculty give his annual praise-and-caution speech in the auditorium afterward. Paul and Tammy sat on her right, appropriately solemn, subvocally sarcastic, keeping a small circle of colleagues in red-faced silent giggles until the meeting was done and they exploded like fools.

Litten scowled, and Mel told him not to be such an old fart. "Good lord, Sam, don't you remember what it was like not to be a part of an enemy?"

"Is that what you think of me, the enemy?"

She stood and made her way out to the aisle. "No, not at all. It just seems to me there are times—like all the time, Sam—when you take this job, and life, too seriously. Things are beautiful, Sam. And there's fun to be had. I don't mean party-type fun, but just . . . well, enjoyment of things." She glanced at him a little sadly. "Sometimes I think you don't see that at all."

In the large crescent lobby—reds and golds and a swirled marble floor—she rose on her toes to search over the heads of the milling crowd, hoping the Prescotts had not deserted her, leaving her to Sam. Paul she could see near the blind-faced ticket windows on the far side; Tammy, she guessed, had gone to the ladies' room. When Paul finally spotted her he lifted an inquiring eyebrow, and she nodded. He grinned. Winked. And Sam bulled his way to her side and touched her waist.

"Your problem, Melissa," he said as if they had not stopped talking, "is that you don't take enough seriously."

"Is this my chairman talking, or my friend?"

He put a hand to his ascot and untied it absently. "Both, I suppose."

She looked hard at him then, slightly puzzled. He had never spoken to her this way before—sober tones veiling possible threats—and she wasn't sure she knew how to handle it. However, neither was she about to permit him to ruin the good mood that had returned with her baiting him. The day was too nice, and the vacation too near. Instead, she told him she would be in tomorrow for just an hour or two to hand in her examinations for copying, then she would be gone for the holidays. With the student body already scattered and her work caught up, she didn't think he would mind. The disappointment that crumpled his face was almost heartbreaking, and she felt herself about ready to do something stupid when Paul suddenly loomed over them and reminded her of a nonexistent date she had with him and his wife.

The parting was swift, Litten close to surly, and ten minutes later they were in the Prescott's station wagon and heading back into the village. The snow had thickened somewhat, had nearly covered the dead brown ground, and the gentle silence that came with it eased her, made her smile.

The windshield wipers thumped rhythmically.

The heater, though set low, made all of them drowsily quiet.

"Sam looks to be getting awfully pushy," Paul said at last.

"I'm used to it," Mel told him.

"You never needed rescuing before."

She explained quickly what had disturbed her, left her nearly vulnerable to Sam's advances, then pointed suddenly across Tammy toward the other side of the road. "There," she said. "You can see it back in there."

Tammy nodded thoughtfully. "Yeah. Yeah, I can see what you mean. Doesn't look so bad now, though. With all the snow on it, I mean."

"You should have seen it before. My god, when I thought that guy was really following me I almost had a heart attack."

"No clue as to who he is?" Paul said without taking his eyes from the road.

"Nope."

"Well," Tammy said, shifting just enough so that Mel had to slide closer to the door, "if you ask me—and I'm not saying you are—I think the two of you are making an awful lot out of nothing. Mel sees some guy by the house on Friday and he spooks her, right? So she walks to school and thinks a tree stump is the same man, right? And poor dear Sam's got so much hots for her that she's ready to climb the walls because he's also her boss and she doesn't know what to do about it. Right? Seems simple to me. You're cracking up, kid." She grinned. "Think about it." And laughed.

Mel didn't object to the crack, nor the odd way Tammy looked at her while she hugged briefly her husband's arm. Probably, she decided, Tammy was right. And the man in the raincoat was probably one of her students, trying to figure a way to either spook her (and somehow affect the finals) or make a not very subtle pass.

Or maybe she hadn't seen the guy at all. It was dark and she had been drinking and . . . hell, who the hell cares?

At Centre Street the Prescotts let her out so she could do some idle shopping before returning home. The sun was already down, the air tinged a faint shade of lilac, and she kept her hands deep in her pockets as she walked through the village's only business district. Grinning. Sometimes humming. Losing herself at last in the freshly minted holiday spirit brought on by the new snow that laced the bare trees at the curbing, brightened the strings of lights in shopwindows, softened the pedestrians' footsteps on the somewhat slippery pavement. Quiet carols chimed from a speaker above the National Bank's entrance. Children, bundled and red-cheeked, shoe-skied on the sidewalk. She breathed deeply, still grinning, greeted several people she knew with hugs and solid kisses.

Lovely, she thought as a flake nestled on an eyelash. Oxrun in winter is nothing less than heaven.

And when, by accident, she found herself standing next to the library, looking across the street at the pine-greens-bedecked post office, there was only the slightest twinge of melancholy at being the last of her family. Only the slightest. Because life, her life, was still filled with joy.

She laughed aloud, turned around and headed back down the street without any urge to hurry. Lingering. Listening. Once ducking away from a kid-thrown snowball. Every so often an automobile with chains on its tires chattered past, the sound reminding her of sleighs and harness bells. She stuck out her tongue to taste a snowflake, stared for what seemed like hours at jewelry in display windows and eventually returned home with nothing in her arms and not the least bit disappointed.

She showered quickly and changed into slacks and a sweater, then considered calling Sam, thinking that somehow she ought to apologize for her abrupt departure with Paul, and for something else that she didn't quite understand. But the line was busy, and the decision vanished, and she buried herself in her study to finish cutting the stencils for her classes' exams.

It took her almost three hours, with no more break than it took to make herself a sandwich and a cup of coffee. Not eating, she told herself, was good for the figure.

When she was finished, she stood with both hands massaging the small of her back and realized that the house was dark. Her first thought was for the tree lights, and she stumbled into the living room and switched them on. Smiled softly at the reflections in the decorations, in the bow window, and hummed tunelessly to herself as she reached out to palm away condensation on one of the panes.

And the man in black was standing under the streetlamp.

She stood in the still-dark room, telephone to hand, peering around the bulk of the tree.

"I *know*, Michael, I *know*," she whispered, as though the figure might overhear her. "But he isn't *doing* anything. He's just *standing* there, looking at the house. At least I *think* he's looking at the house. I can't really tell. I can't see his face."

"Just call the police, Melissa. I'll be over in five minutes."

"But what if he leaves before they get here?"

A sigh of scarce tolerance. "Melissa, it doesn't matter if he's still there or not. You give them a description and let them do the rest."

"Oh, great. There's a man out there in a black hat and a black raincoat and I can't see his face or his hands or his feet. What am I supposed to tell the cops?"

"That."

She exhaled loudly. "Michael, that doesn't make any sense."

"And you aren't making any sense tying up the phone when you could be calling the police."

"Michael—"

"Do it, Melissa. I'm on my way."

She replaced the receiver with an exasperated sigh and set the unit on the floor. One strand of tree lights winked at her. A small red bulb swayed. With one hand extended to guard against table corners she made her way across the room into the foyer, pressed herself to the front door and looked through the single rectangular pane set vertically into the wood at eye level.

The man was gone.

Instantly, she grabbed a coat from the hall rack and rushed outside, ignoring the snow clinging wetly to her hair and neck, elbows tucked against her waist as she moved as quickly as she dared down toward the light. She could see no one in either direction, heard no doors closing, no car's ignition grinding.

And when she came to where the figure had been standing, there were no footprints in the snow.

The couch was small, virtually a love seat, but it was set against the room's rear wall facing the tree, and the lights comforted her more than Michael's pacing. He still wore his topcoat, his hat darkly wet, and when he spoke she felt as though she were a jury addressed instead of a lover pacified.

"You know how hard you've been working, Mel. I'm not at all surprised you're—"

"Seeing things?"

He paused, glanced at her, resumed his pacing. "I wasn't going to say that, love. I was going to say, I'm not surprised you're making mountains out of mole-hills."

"Moles don't usually make a habit of casing my house."

"Melissa, Melissa," he said. "There are days when I

just don't know what I'm going to do with you."

"Try flopping down in my lap and I'll show you."

He pushed his glasses to the end of his nose and peered at her over the top. She stuck her tongue out at him and faked a stubborn pout.

"Melissa," he said. Sighed. Said "Melissa" again.

Mel resigned herself to a long chorus of her name, not to mention a verse or two about how she was a scientist and should be more careful with her observations. She knew all the signs; she had been faced with them often. Try as he might (and she knew that he tried), Michael simply could not get over the fact that she had actually managed to conquer the fear that had given her nightmares when she'd first returned—the fear that whoever had killed her mother and those other men would someday return to kill her, too.

Paul, a practicing psychiatrist as well as an author and classroom lecturer, had told her this wasn't exactly the most normal of reactions; on the other hand, considering the circumstances of her mother's death (and the deaths of her two brothers, however unrelated), it was understandable. He had worked with her for several months (unofficially and at his office), finally convincing her that the dreams and the fear would vanish immediately she grasped how farfetched her fear was.

He had been right.

It was gone, as well as the dreams.

For two years she had slept without waking with a scream, had been able to walk into the post office without almost blacking out.

But what in bloody hell had happened to those footprints? Unless, she thought suddenly, the man had been standing off the curb, in the gutter. It *was* dark. And he had been wearing black. And suddenly she felt incredibly stupid.

Before she could say anything, however, Michael stopped his pensive wandering and stepped around the cobbler's bench she kept in front of the couch. He shoved aside a low pile of magazines and sat, throwing his coat away from his knees, clasping his hands and rocking them for emphasis. "Mel, I may only be a country lawyer, you know—"

For god's sake, stop fishing for compliments, she thought at him, one of the few faults she'd discovered in him thus far.

"—but I do manage to learn something about people's reactions to stress."

"Stress?" She frowned, puzzled and not at all liking the tone of his voice. "What stress are you talking about, Mike? This house is all paid for, I get a regular—but not spectacular—paycheck, and I like living in the Station better than anyplace else I've been in the world. What in god's name kind of stress are you talking about? That man out there? He's a kid. I just figured it out. He's just a kid trying to scare me."

He cleared his throat perfunctorily. "Just what I'm talking about. Ordinarily, something like that wouldn't bother you, would it. On the other hand, I should tell you Tammy called me at the office after they let you off this afternoon."

"Oh . . . damn," she said to the ceiling.

"Mel, you have to take this more seriously."

She grimaced. "That's what Sam said, too."

"You know what I mean."

She pushed herself into the corner and drew her legs up beneath her. "I know what you mean," she said curtly. "And I don't think Sam's amorous attentions are putting more stress on me than . . . than any one of a dozen students of mine who are dying to find out what I wear under my lab coat."

"But they are your students," he pointed out. "Sam is your boss. You'll be up for tenure at the end of next term, and if Sam gives you thumbs down, you'll—"

"He won't." She shook her head emphatically. "He wouldn't do that to me."

Michael shrugged. "Maybe he will, maybe he won't. But Mel, you've got to at least consider the possibility that your job is more tied up with his making passes at you than you think."

She opened her mouth to protest, closed it when acceptance of Michael's suggestion reached her before she was ready. "It's almost enough to make me start smoking again," she whispered, uncurled and reached for him awkwardly. He took her shoulders and kissed her, stroked her hair, brushed a thumb over each of her eyes in a gesture that had begun eight months ago, when they'd first met and he'd tried unsuccessfully to sweep hair from her face. It was a warm move, a silent and eloquent one that never failed to bring her peace.

"Are you jealous?" she asked with her eyes still closed.

She could hear a laugh bubbling deep in his throat, felt a momentary disappointment when he said that he wasn't. Well, you should be, she thought. Though she wasn't any more vain than most people were, she also knew she would get no sympathy at all protesting that she was plain, unpretty, not worthy of attention. She knew (or suspected) how attractive she really was; but unlike Tammy—perhaps because of her friend's teach-

ing of drama and theater arts—she never made a point
of accentuating looks over skills. At least, she thought
guiltily, not deliberately, not consciously.

"I have to go," Michael said, and kissed her again,
kept his arm about her waist until they reached the front
door. "Don't worry. I think you're right about that kid.
As for Sam . . . well, he can't hurt you unless you let
him."

"But it wasn't Sam I saw out there, Michael."

"Melissa, for pete's sake!"

She laughed and pushed him gently out the door,
waited until he'd driven away before returning inside
and heading for another hot shower and a good night's
sleep. But it wasn't until she was under her blankets and
sighing at the dark that she decided she had better try to
figure out how to cool Sam Litten down without hurting
him, or somehow losing him as a friend. Not that she
believed he would link her tenure with her compliance.
Sam wasn't like that. She knew him too well.

And she cursed at the fingers that were crossed over
her stomach.

Cursed the next morning when she burned the toast
and the coffee and had to leave in a hurry, with nothing
but orange juice turning to acid in her stomach.

Grinning until her cheeks ached when she caught herself checking for prints in the snow. A kid or a figment,
no question about it.

And the stump in the woods was just a stump in the
woods when she drove toward the campus to give her
car a workout. The sun glared, the sky was sharply blue,
and Chancellor Avenue had been plowed to its blacktop. A beautiful day. December. There is nothing, she
thought, like winter in New England.

And she held the thought again when she got out of her car in the faculty parking lot. The buildings were stone-block, arranged in an open-sided rectangle that faced down a gentle slope heavily wooded. The Avenue was nearly a mile away, just visible through the branches, when a passing windshield caught the sun. It was silent here now that the students were gone, the snow undisturbed, icicles under the eaves, boulders like half-completed snowmen spotting the broad quad. "Yes," she whispered, then tucked the packet of stencils under her arm and headed for the two-story brownstone that housed the Science Department—classrooms, eight labs, and an office for each of Sam Litten's charges.

The building was as quiet as the campus outside. But once her hearing adjusted, Mel could identify the muffled mutterings of radiators, the distant clacking of a typewriter, the hum of a vacuum cleaner, probably in the large office where the secretaries worked. Deliberately, then, she kept her heels from cracking on the corridor's worn flooring as she hurried past a row of frosted-glass doors to the one which had her name on it, still gold and gleaming. From her coat pocket she pulled a key ring, fumbled because the stencils were slipping, finally turned the lock over and nudged the door open with a thrust of her hip.

The office was crowded, narrow, and she had to side-step a pile of journals to dump the stencils onto her desk. Sighed loudly and listened for signs of company. When she heard none she smiled. And once out of her coat she gathered the stencils together and took a plastic cafeteria chair closer to the arched window overlooking the quad. She could, she knew, just leave them in the office and let a secretary do the proofing; but she was still too eager to do all the work herself. If there were any mistakes, she wanted them to be hers.

She sat, stretched, pulled the stencils to her lap and started to read.

A shadow passed over her.

She paused. Looked up. Saw nothing out the window but the bright glaring snow. And what if you stood up, she asked herself then; do you think you'd see the man standing under one of the elms?

No, she thought angrily. Because there is no man.

"Melissa," she said aloud, and glad for her voice, "it's time you stopped thinking and did some work for a change." And almost jumped from her chair when someone crossed the threshold.

"My god, Sam, you nearly scared me to death!"

Litten grinned a weak apology. "You sticking around for lunch?"

"No," she said after a moment's hesitation. "I have things to do later."

He nodded. "Oh. Well, if you're sure . . ."

She placed the awkwardly long stencils carefully back on her lap. "I'm sure, Sam."

"I see. Well . . . it's just that I thought . . ." He put a quivering hand to the sweater-vest that covered his paunch, stroked it absently. His tie was off, his jacket unbuttoned, almost as if he'd forgotten to dress completely. "I just thought—"

"Sam," she cautioned, "please don't start, okay?"

"I don't understand."

She felt it immediately—the draining of the sunlight captured in her soul. "Look, just leave it alone, all right? I can't have lunch with you, and that's that. No room for argument."

The brief scowl that twisted across his face alarmed her and she straightened, her back rigid; but as quickly as it appeared it was gone.

"Mel, perhaps we ought to talk about . . . about the upcoming semester, do you think? There's a lot we have to discuss about what you need and—"

His name was almost a growl. "Sam . . . don't push it."

He left her without another word, and she sagged, breathing deeply as she struggled with her annoyance. It wasn't fair, she thought, that someone like that—a dear man, but a pest—could come along and threaten to ruin what was sure to be a perfect day. Didn't the idiot know it was Christmas? Couldn't he see all that snow out there, feel that marvelously cold air? What the hell was he trying to do, make her unhappy just because she would not respond to his pathetic overtures?

She snorted her disgust, turned back to her work and completed it without so much as a single alteration. She no longer cared how tough the questions were, or how fair; Sam had effectively spoiled what good feelings she might have had for her students. They would have to know all the work, it was as simple as that. No gifts. No easy problems. And the more she thought about it the angrier she became. She slammed the stencils onto the windowsill, walked the office for nearly five minutes before slipping back into her coat and heading for the secretaries' room where the duplicating would be done.

No one was there to take her instructions. She glowered at the deserted chairs and scribbled what she wanted done on a black sheet of paper, paper-clipped the mess together and tossed it onto the nearest desk. If they had any complaints, they could just call her at home.

As if they would have more complaints than she did

right now.

Sam, she thought, there are times when I could throttle you.

She paused at the exit, one foot tapping the floor. What she should do now, right now, before things went too far, was to confront the fool and convince him to stay away from her, that they were friends and nothing more. This kind of hassle she simply did not need at all; and before she could think about it she was striding purposefully down the corridor, eyes narrowed, hair flaring back over her shoulders.

Her heels, loud.

The building, quiet.

Sunlight in square puddles, shimmering on the floor.

She flung open Litten's door . . . and stopped as if a glass wall had been thrown up before her.

The room, not much larger than her own but longer, was a shambles: books, periodicals, pamphlets, stacks of paper and notebooks had been dragged down from the shelves that lined the walls, a large typewriter and its metal stand had been toppled into the far corner, and through the open window drifted large melting flakes that stained the wall beneath and made dark the worn fringed carpet.

A movement, and she looked sharply to her left, saw the ancient maple desk Litten had dragged here during the summer, and over it the struggling figures of the darkman and Sam.

Sam was on the bottom, his hands flailing the air, his thighs pinned hard to the flat of the desk. She could see his face blanched and running red, could see from the sleeves of the black raincoat narrow glittering claws that raked through Sam's sweater and laid bare his ribs. And still Sam fought, mouth gasping (all of it in silence), fingers working to pry the darkman loose (no sound, no sound at all). He arched his back abruptly and almost wriggled free, one knee coming up between the darkman's legs swiftly and hard . . . and completely without effect. The claws rose, fell, rose again and splattered rosebuds of blood onto the windowsill, onto the walls. Rose. Fell. And Sam's nose was split from eye to upper lip.

(all of it in silence, not even the breathing)

Mel staggered back into the corridor, hands pressed white-knuckled to her mouth. Her first scream was a gagging that sent her into a tight, weaving spin. The second thrust her against the opposite wall. The third trailed weakly after her as she collapsed to the floor, knees up, hands at her sides, her lips pale and her eyes filled with tears.

And no matter how hard she tried, she could not lose consciousness, or release the fourth scream.

She never really got over it, you know. She hid it pretty well, but she never really shook it.

So you keep telling me.

So what do you think, Paul? Was it bound to happen, because of her family?

I don't know what you're talking about. Was what bound to happen?

You know . . . this breakdown, or whatever the term is.

Mike, sometimes I wonder where in hell your brain is. What?

Breakdown. I'm talking about breakdowns. Nervous breakdowns.

*Well, what about them? Are you saying . . . are you
trying to tell me she hasn't had one? That this isn't a
breakdown?*

*Of course it isn't, you idiot. No. I'm sorry, I take that
back. But honest to god, Mike, I wish you'd remember
who's the lawyer and who's the doctor around here. I've
enough troubles with Tammy as it is already.*

All right, all right. I'm sorry too.

go away

*No problem. But the first thing is, you can't go
around telling people Mel's had a breakdown. She
hasn't. She's only reacting to what she saw, and you
have to admit it isn't everyone who walks into an office
and finds a dead body. Especially when that dead body
belongs to one of your best friends.*

*But she kept mumbling about that guy in the rain-
coat!*

*Sure she did. She has to externalize in some way,
Mike. She saw a shadow, and she saw Sam sprawled
back over the desk like that, and the first thing her mind
did was connect the shadow to the man she thought she
saw outside the house at the party. She's already done
this once, you know. She thought a tree stump was the
man. It was on her way to work yesterday.*

go away . . . please?

Twice, Paul.

Huh?

Twice. She saw him twice at the house.

When?

*The party was the first time, last night was the
second. She called me when she saw him, but when I got
there he was gone. She thinks it was probably a student
playing a prank, but I think he wasn't there at all. She*

showed me where he was supposed to have been, but there weren't any footprints. The snow was deep enough, but there weren't any footprints.

I'll be damned.

I told her to call the police, see, and then I got right over. I thought it was for real.

go

Did she?

Sure she thought it was real. She called me, didn't she?

away

No; I mean, did she call the police?

Mel? She never does anything I tell her. It's principle, or something. She's as stubborn as her mother was supposed to be. Why do you ask?

Just as well she didn't call. That means this guy in the coat business is just between the four of us.

Hell of a Christmas, isn't it.

Tell me something I don't already know, Mike. Nuts, look at the time. I have to get back out to the college and pick up Tammy at the theater. Auditorium. Whatever the hell they call it when they work there. She has a bunch of her Barrymores practicing again. I tell you, Mike, I don't know how they put up with her.

Because she's good, Paul. She's damned good.

"Damnit, go away!"

She heard shuffling, a changing of positions, and felt a hand cover hers on the bed. Her bed.

"Mel?" It was Paul.

She didn't want to open her eyes. It was nice where she was; it was snowing again outside and there were wreaths on all the doors and Sam was still chasing after her in his own, wonderfully clumsy way.

"Mel, come on, you can't hide in there forever."

"Oh yes I can."

The two men laughed quietly.

"Mike?"

"Right here, Mel."

She felt her other hand covered, turned it over and squeezed his tightly. "Sam . . . is he . . ."

"A massive coronary," Paul said. "From what we can gather, he was trying to lift that stupid typewriter when it hit him." A pause. "It was quick, Mel. He was gone before he hit the desk."

It wasn't quick, she thought. It was slow. It was painful. He was torn apart and he was bleeding . . . she felt herself drifting, recalling then that someone, a doctor (Paul?) had given her a shot once Mike had brought her home. She wouldn't have the hospital; she had insisted on her own house, her own bed, and no one had argued.

Drifting . . .

"I have to leave now, Mel. Tammy sends you her love."

She tried to nod but the effort was too great. Instead, her eyelids fluttered, stilled when she felt him kiss her forehead. A moment later she heard him leave, another minute and the front door closed.

"Mike?"

"I haven't left, love. In fact, I'm going to sleep in the spare room."

"That bed's lumpy. Use the couch."

"Mel, I'm six four. That thing will cramp me for life."

She grinned. Sweet Michael. How sweet Michael is.

She wanted to speak his name, but the drifting snared her.

She had no dreams. But when she woke the next morning the man in the black raincoat was standing in the driveway.

She wanted to duck away from the window, to hide behind the curtains and examine the darkman without him seeing her.

She did not move.

She placed her palms on the sill and leaned forward, squinting against the sun's glare off the snow. There was a fascination, fearful and exciting, and she had to know who the kid was, who the man was, before she screamed for Michael to get the police.

The scream never came.

A cloud sifted the sunlight from gold to grey, and she could see through the darkman to the shrubbery behind him.

When she woke again it was late afternoon, the house was silent and gooseflesh had broken out over her arms. She shivered as she remembered stumbling back to the bed, but did not know if it was the drug or her fear that had driven her to sleep. She yawned and rubbed her arms. Slipped off the mattress and pulled a bathrobe from her closet, covering the nightgown that rustled barely to her knees. Mules with pink tassels warmed her feet. She wondered who had undressed her—Michael, or Paul. Then, when she could think of nothing else to stop her, she walked to the window . . . and the darkman was gone.

Enough, she thought, annoyed to exasperation. This is quite enough, thank you.

When she checked the spare room, Michael was gone,

a note on the pillow telling her he would call her tonight. Or come over if she wanted.

She didn't.

She wanted to be alone. She needed time to think.

Down in the kitchen she made herself some coffee and sat at a tiny round table with the cup between her palms. Twilight made the house seem cold, and she worked the collar of her robe close around her neck. The furnace grumbled on in the cellar. A draught kissed her ankles, and she crossed them under the chair.

One step at a time, she told herself then; let's take this nonsense one step at a time.

Number One: Somebody was watching her, following her, and she didn't think now that it had anything to do with any of her students. She didn't know why; it was a feeling, nothing more.

Number Two: It wasn't a ghost. The fact that she had seen through the darkman this morning was conclusive of nothing except that the light was bright and she was still woozy from the sedative. And she had already decided he'd been standing in the gutter, which is why she and Michael found no prints on the ground.

Number Three: It was as unnerving as hell; nevertheless, she did not feel threatened. Again, she didn't know why. The darkman had done nothing but watch her, at a distance, not even bothering to reveal his face.

Number Four: The darkman killed Sam.

Slowly, she lowered the cup to the table and bit at the inside of her cheek. She reached around behind her to the counter and picked up the jar of instant coffee, reached again and grabbed the kettle. The water was tepid, but she drank it anyway.

It killed Sam Litten.

There had been no shadow (as she'd heard Paul say), and the evidence of the struggle had been all over the room. Somehow, in some way, that had all been set right—except for the typewriter—before help arrived.

It *had* killed Sam.

And now Sam's body was flying back to his family in South Carolina, and tomorrow there would be a service in the chapel. She wouldn't go. Nothing could make her listen to the pieties and the homilies without her remembering those claws, that blood . . .

Which brought her to Number Five: She had lied when she told Michael she wasn't under any stress. She was. And most of it, she knew, was stress of her own making. Since she had returned to the Station she had done nothing but try to make those who remembered her mother and her dying forget it all in the brilliance of her own achievements. She was also trying to show them how damned happy she was, in spite of the past, in spite of the fact that her brothers were buried in the Memorial Park on the other side of town. This, plus Sam and those tenure threats of his (recognized at last for what they had really been), was enough to send anyone round the bend, over the edge, into the deep, down into the dark.

It was possible, then, that she might be going crazy. From Paul she knew full well that saying you're crazy really meant you were sane was nothing more than a myth. It was possible, then, she was. Or at least staggering on her way.

And the darkman would be the outward symptom of whatever psychosis her stress was brewing.

Paranoia. The feeling that somewhere out there someone was trying to do you harm.

The trouble was, the darkman wasn't. She already knew that. He wasn't trying to hurt her.

The telephone rang, and the cup slipped from her fingers to shatter on the floor. She stared at it for several rings until it became little more than a bright yellow blob clinging to the wall next to the refrigerator. Then she rose, stepping around the shards of ironstone, pushing aside a chair, reaching for the receiver.

A voice said: *Be happy, Melissa.*

And the dial tone burred.

An hour later it rang again.

Be happy, Melissa. Be happy. Be happy.

She wanted to say, "Who are you?" but again she heard the dial tone, and a faint crackling on the line.

When Michael called at nine she told him she was fine, that she was going to bed, and tomorrow she would be going over to Harley to pick out a last-minute gift for Tammy and Paul. He queried again, and again she reassured him. And when he rang off she went into the study to find a bottle of wine.

When the phone rang at midnight she slapped it off the hook. Stumbled up the steps to her bed and fell on the quilt. She belched, hiccoughed, and thought "paranoia" once more. But what kind of a threat was *be happy, Melissa?*

Thursday Mel did as she promised Michael: she took the car and drove to Harley and bought gifts for her friends. Then she spent the rest of the day riding through the Connecticut countryside, marveling at what the snow had done to the fields, to the hills, to the houses and barns almost too perfect for pictures. She crossed the line into Massachusetts and had lunch at an inn. Swept back into her home state bloated, red-cheeked, and listening to Handel on her car's FM.

It was full dark by the time she reached Quentin Avenue, and her mood had grown so cheerful she was even ready to kiss the darkman. But apparently the ride was exactly what she needed: there were no shadows or blobs or blotches in the air. Only Michael's car at the curb, and Michael waiting on the porch.

She gave him no time for scolding. She grabbed him, kissed him, brought him inside, and they sat in front of the television until Christmas was official. Then they opened their gifts (his to her, gloves; hers to him, a cashmere scarf) and ate a leisurely meal before going to bed.

At dawn he tried to persuade her to come with him to spend the day in Hartford. His parents would love her, he insisted, and they'd love to have her join them. But the day was too special. She wasn't at all sure this was the time for them to examine her, prod her, poke into her past and listen to her speculate on her future. That would have to come at an ordinary time; just in case, she told him, they did not approve.

Michael pouted, grumbled, fumbled into his clothes and told her he wouldn't be returning until Sunday. Would she call him? No; but he'd better call her or his life would be in danger. He laughed and left her, and just before nine she called Paul Prescott to see if the invitation was still open, and she was welcome.

The Prescotts lived on High Street, just off Mainland Road. Their home was new by the Station's standards, and the living room was long, narrow, everything in such extremes of decor that the red brick fireplace with its gilded glass screen seemed just about perfect. Mel sat in a canvas-slung chair and watched with less contentment than she would have wished as Paul fussed expertly with pine logs and kindling, and Tammy made one of her interminable adjustments to the tinsel on the aluminum tree. Two large speakers, affixed deep in the vaulted ceiling, whispered seasonal music to the overly warm air. She listened to it for a while, then slowly (so slowly she would have sworn it was the room moving and not her) turned her head to look out the picture window. Much of the snow had gone, or had turned to black-grey slush at the curbs, but enough stubbornly remained on shrubs and tree bark to give the morning its proper traditional touch.

A swoop of children raced by, dragging behind them freshly waxed sleds. A car honked at them, and they waved, their shrill laughter just audible as they rounded the corner and vanished.

"More, dear?"

Mel glanced down at the teacup in her hand, blinked, then looked up at Tammy and shook her head with a grin. "No, thanks. I think I've had enough to float a Liberty ship."

Tammy smiled quickly (nervously? Mel wondered) and hurried out of the room. Mel watched her leave, then looked to Paul, whose back was still toward her, muttering to himself because his matches wouldn't light. He yanked hard at his mustache, shook a fist at the logs, and it was all Mel could do to keep from laughing. And that made her frown. Ordinarily, she would have laughed, would have teased Paul unmercifully, and Tammy would have joined her. But though neither had said anything directly to her, she could tell the moment she walked through the door that in the time it had taken her to dress and drive over the invitation had . . . not quite soured, but lost its hearty welcome.

Neither of them had said anything to her about her collapse at school, or of the service she had skipped. In fact, Sam's name hadn't been mentioned at all. So what was the matter, her irritation demanded; did they think she was crazy or something, that she would contaminate them both? She would have killed, then, to know what Paul had told his wife about the darkman.

And that was something else that had not been mentioned.

It could have been the holiday, of course. This was hardly the time to talk about matters unpleasant and minds near unbalanced. But somehow she didn't think that was the case here at all.

Tammy returned, then—bright in black leotards edged with silver, with an overskirt of green that *hushed* when she walked—and broke into the ceremony of exchanging their gifts.

Her present was an exquisite gold compact engraved with her name; Tammy's a lamb's-wool coat; Paul's a volume of Dickens' short stories. And they laughed more than necessary when she realized she'd left her own presents at home.

"Absentminded," Paul said to her, grinning and chuckling. "The stereotype reborn, right here in this very house."

"It's a far, far better thing you do," Tammy said, one arm flung high, the other across her face. "It was probably toilet water."

"Hey," she said, "don't knock it. It was fresh from my tap."

Laughter again, until Mel saw Paul virtually fondling

his book. "Do you watch that movie every year, *A Christmas Carol*, I mean?"

"Are you kidding?" Tammy said. "Every chance he gets. He's an expert, you know. Just ask him to explain which is the better Scrooge, Alistair Sim or Reginald Owen." Paul blushed, and Mel blew him a kiss. "And every time poor Tiny Tim dies, when you see the crutches there by the fireplace, you know what I mean? Every time that happens, the old sot cries."

"I most certainly do not," he said, though he smiled over the denial.

"I'll bet you do, too," Mel accused with a laugh. "And ten to one you're scared to death of the Ghost of Christmas to Come."

Tammy scoffed. "Nuts. That man there isn't afraid of anything. I tell you, Mel, he's no fun at horror movies, no fun at all."

"Not even when there're ghosts?"

"No such thing," Paul said. "Not, that is, if you mean people who've died and have come back to haunt us." He frowned, then, and looked at her sideways. "Why? Are you seeing ghosts, Mel?"

"Hey, Paul, come on!" Tammy said. "It's Christmas, for crying out loud."

"No," Mel said. Then she tried to find a way to get comfortable in the chair, surrendered with a shrug and slid to the floor, where she crossed her legs and lay her hands on her knees. She was wearing a green blouse and dark slacks, was fully aware that her position drew the material snug over her curves. Was aware, too, that Paul didn't miss a rounding. "But isn't that the only kind there are?"

"Nope. You've got the mind kind, too."

"The mind kind?"

"He means," Tammy said, "the kind that people think they see but are only in their minds. Guilt, desire, stuff like that. Now can we stop talking about it?"

"Is that what you mean, Paul?" she said.

When he nodded she felt ice at the back of her neck.

Still felt it after lunch and almost didn't hear Paul excuse himself from the table. But when they were alone, she saw Tammy looking hard at her, and not at all kindly.

"What?" she said.

Tammy, flustered, began fussing with her hair. "Nothing, really. I was just wondering something, that's all."

Mel smiled. In spite of the ice, in spite of the setback, she'd not had a more pleasant day in weeks. Nothing, she thought, could spoil her present mood. "Come on, dear, what's bothering you?"

"If you must know . . . you are."

Mel wasn't sure she had heard her friend clearly. "Me? Are you talking about me?"

"We've been married nearly fourteen years, you know," Tammy said, taking a fork and twirling it slowly in her hands. "It isn't my fault we couldn't have children, but he never seemed to mind. He had his work, and I had the stage, and everything seemed to be moving along just great, you know what I mean?" She put the fork down, picked up a spoon. "About two years ago he started staying late at the office, both downtown and at the college. He was still writing that book, so I didn't think anything of it. But . . . well, it just hasn't been the same between us. There's a distance there, Mel, and I don't know how to cross it." The spoon fell to the carpet, and she took hold of a knife. She smiled wanly. "He talks a lot about you and Mike, you know. He thinks you'll make the perfect pair once you get together. Is it going to be soon, Mel? Have you set the date yet?"

The ice slid around to her chest, penetrated and took hold of her lungs, her heart. The brightness of the room dimmed, and the twinkling of the snow outside became nothing more than a glare.

"Tammy," she said quietly, "there isn't anything to worry about."

"I . . . god, I hope not."

"There never was."

Tammy pushed away from the table and walked out of the room, but Mel discovered that her legs would not work. She wanted to stand, but neither her arms nor her knees wanted to cooperate. *But it's Christmas, damnit*! she wanted to call out; *what the hell are you talking about, me and Paul*! *What the hell are you talking about*?

The words would not come. She could only sit there, gripping hard the edge of the table, watching her friend slump sadly to the floor in front of the fireplace and stare forlornly at the flames that snapped at the chimney. Sand crawled into her eyes, and she rubbed them hard with her knuckles. She could not believe it; she was invited into this house, and suddenly, without any warning, accused of having an affair with a friend who happened to be the husband of a friend.

What was wrong with everyone today?

Don't they know what day it is?

First Paul gave her those looks when he was talking about ghosts (and admittedly it was a dumb thing to bring up in the first place), and now there was Tammy. There was something more to this; there had to be. They'd known each other too long for such childish nonsense to come between them like this. My god, wasn't it Paul and Tammy—and especially Tammy— who'd helped her get started when she'd come back to Oxrun? Wasn't it Tammy who showed her the ropes, the politics, the hazards in each department? What kind of game was she playing? It occurred to her that perhaps Tammy wasn't really happy with Paul at all and was searching for an excuse—it didn't matter which one, which kind—any excuse to get out from under. But that didn't wash either. If there had been any tension, any signs of breaking, she would have noticed something long before now.

Paul stepped into the living room, looked at his wife, looked to Mel and took several paces toward her.

"What," he asked, "did you say to Tammy."

"Nothing," she said flatly. "I said nothing at all." As Paul turned away she stopped him with his name. "She, on the other hand, wanted to know if we were still . . . seeing each other. On the sly, as it were."

He was looking back over his shoulder. "I don't believe it."

"Ask her."

"Mel, what's bothering you?" He returned and leaned his hands on the table, his elbows locked. "Are you seeing that guy in black again, is that what it is? Did you say something to her about it?"

She denied it with a crisp shake of her head, denied it again when his expression told her he still didn't believe it. It *was* that bad around here, then, she realized; they were in fact having trouble and she had been too blind, or too pollyanna, to see it. Quickly, she pulled her napkin off her lap and dropped it on the table, rose and walked to the front closet.

"Where are you going?" Paul said, standing directly behind her.

"Home," she told him. "If I stay here any longer, I'll just ruin everyone's Christmas."

He appeared ready to take hold of her shoulders, but a look into the living room stayed him. "Mel, I think you'd better call me tomorrow."

She pulled away from his helping hand and shrugged into her coat unassisted, tied her scarf carelessly over her hair and knotted it tightly under her chin. "No, I don't think I will."

"Mel, you can't fool me. You have been seeing that man again."

Point Number Five: She could be going crazy.

She almost told him, had the words arranged and ready, but a sudden fanfare from the ceiling speakers stopped her. "You'd better see to Tammy."

"Mel, you're being foolish." He followed her to the end of the porch, his grasp just missing her shoulder as she hurried down the steps. "Mel! Mel, you need help."

She paused at the juncture of slate walk and pavement, saw the aluminum tree glittering through the window, saw Tammy's shadow in front of the fire. "Just leave it, Paul, okay? I'm all right. There's nothing to worry about."

She was into the car before he could speak again, away from the curb and heading for home before she realized how violently she was trembling. Beneath a rakish cap a snowman winked at her from his perch in someone's yard. She slowed as she passed it, taking deep breaths that did nothing to calm her. It was frustrating; she didn't know whether to be afraid or angry, whether to lock herself in the house or drive straight to Hartford and demand that Michael do something about her.

Her palms slapped mindlessly at the steering wheel. She sucked her lips between her teeth and tried to bring herself pain.

And as she pulled into the driveway, the darkman vanished around the back corner of the house.

The car bucked as it stopped, grinding into a stall, but she was out the door and running, leaving the keys in the ignition. The melted snow had formed ice puddles near the base of the house, and one of them nearly sent her sprawling into a clutch of burlap-hooded rose bushes. Something twisted behind her left knee. Lurching, now, to keep her balance, she flung her hands out to the house and propelled herself into the back yard . . . stopped with a windmilling, agonizing skid.

The cherry trees in back, the glass-sided feeder to the left of the low fence that marked her neighor's property, the handle of a rake poking out of a drift alongside the garage. Nothing more. She had not been out here since the snowfall; except for a few splayed bird tracks, the white was unbroken.

Point Number Six: There was no gutter to stand in here; the darkman doesn't exist.

She kept her mind as blank as possible as she dropped her coat onto the floor beside the couch. Yanked off the scarf and wadded it into a ball to toss at the baseboard. Sat and pulled off her shoes, throwing them to the carpet to hear their thumping, watch them roll toward the empty Christmas presents. Her hands massaged her feet to get them warm, pulled her blouse out from her slacks so she could scratch at her stomach without undoing the buttons.

Then she pulled a fistful of hair over her shoulder and combed it with her fingers until it was dark.

Point Number Seven.

Sitting in the black. The streetlamp backlighting the tree, making it solid, turning the ribbon bows into wings and the bulbs to shrunken heads. Hiding the corners, shrinking the room, forcing her to lift her feet to the cushion in case there were tigers prowling the floor. Listening to the furnace, wondering if it had legs to scuttle it, lumber it, slide it across the cellar floor to the raw-wood steps that led to the kitchen; listening to the warm air seep through the vents, swirling the dust, poking at the ruffled skirt of the chair near the study, filling the room with the touch of spider legs. Sitting in the dark. Feeling the perspiration roll down her temples, glide down her jaw, bubble at her nape, roll down her spine to the roll at her waist, slip to her buttocks, darken her slacks; feeling the saliva force her to swallow; feeling the single tear force her to blink. Sitting in the dark. Her hands on her thighs feeling the muscles jumping, feeling the cloth that covered her skin, feeling the heat that rose from her groin, feeling the tension that made stiff her arms, feeling the air and the sweat and the spiders. Swallowing. Listening. Feeling. Touching. Sitting in the dark until the moon rose and brought silver to the room, gave the tree shape, gave the corners depth, rid the carpet of its tigers, rid the air of the spiders.

An inhalation that took a full minute to fill her lungs. Exhaling through her mouth with a soft hissing whistle. Inhaling. Whistling. Inhaling. Whistling.

An inch. One inch. A shadow at a time she moved her left foot to the edge of the cushion. Let it dangle. Let it descend, one inch, one shadow, until her sole brushed the carpet.

An inch. One inch. A shadow at a time she moved her right foot to the edge of the cushion. Let it dangle. Let it descend, one inch, one shadow, until her sole brushed the carpet.

Outside. In the distance. Sirens . . . sirens.

Outside. On the sidewalk. Voices . . . quiet voices.

While her right hand slowly unbuttoned her blouse (it must be time for bed; there's no light in the air), she rose and padded over to the tree. It was snowing again, small flakes, playing with the breeze that turned them to dervishes with streaming white tails. People on the sidewalk. She counted nine in all: four adults and five youngsters with ski hats and mufflers and topcoats and two lanterns and papers in their hands that fluttered against the wind. A sneeze. A giggling. A ragged start, then a song. Harmony now, not perfect, not wrong. A door across the street sent gold to the snow, and figures on the threshold stood warmly to listen. A window was opened. A car stopped in the street. The carolers walked onward, their lanterns aloft.

Outside. In the distance. Sirens . . . sirens.

She ran into the dining room and pressed face and palms to the panes, straining to hear the last note of the singing, catch the last light of the lantern, wondering

who it was who would spend Christmas night away
from their homes.

Not that it mattered. It had started her smiling, and
once she felt the pull of her lips she held it, and held it,
and hummed to herself as she walked up the stairs. Sang
several noëls as she turned on the shower and stripped
off her clothes. Looked at the razor, and looked at her
legs.

All in all, she thought as she stepped into the stall, she
was handling her madness reasonably well. All it had
taken was a simple act of banishment, and a simple act
of fear. And once done, she was able to sweep out the
confusion that had been stalking her since that party last
week. One week ago. One week tonight.

She had no more questions now, everything was answered. She didn't have to worry about footprints in the
snow or shadows under streetlamps or creatures with
claws that mauled her good friends. She didn't have to
worry. She could handle it. She could accept it.

What she needed to do now, she thought as she
toweled herself dry and brushed at her hair, was get into
bed and try to sleep without dreams. In the morning she
would call Prescott and explain what she'd concluded,
then call Michael and make sure that his Christmas had
been all right.

She frowned.

Michael. With the towel saronged about her she
hurried into the bedroom and looked at the digital clock
on the nightstand. Almost midnight. Why hadn't he
called her? He promised he would.

She took a slow breath (that whistled out slowly) and
decided that she wouldn't let it bother her, not now. She
had too much to worry about. She had herself above all

to keep from shattering; and as long as she could hold on until Paul came to save her then nothing else could touch her. Later, perhaps, but not now. Not now.

The confusion was over, and tomorrow she would mend.

She smiled, giggled when her stomach grumbled and reminded her she hadn't eaten since lunch. A hesitation, a brushing back of the quilt so she could slip in later, and she made her way downstairs, through the foyer, through the dark. Toast and orange juice. A pungent cup of tea. Not looking at the windows, not looking at the doors. Upstairs again and her head on the pillow. Sighing. Sighing. Thinking: Melissa, don't worry, you're handling it quite well.

At midnight the telephone: *Merry Christmas, Melissa.*

The voice wasn't Michael's.

By ten-thirty the next morning she had vacuumed the entire first floor, washed the dishes, scrubbed the kitchen floor, picked up the needles that had fallen from the tree, polished the dining room table, swept the snow from the porch, shoveled the driveway, brushed the snow from the car, showered and washed her hair, scrubbed the bathtub and toilet, changed the linen and made the bed, vacuumed the entire second floor, dusted the window seat, washed her hands, changed the linen in the spare room and made the bed, and was standing on the landing wondering what else she could do before she called Paul when the telephone rang.

She almost fell as she ran down the stairs, forced herself to hold her chin up, keep her back straight, eyes dead ahead as she walked into the kitchen and picked up the receiver.

"Merry Christmas, Melissa!"

"Michael?"

"I tried to call you last night but you didn't answer the phone. Did you stay at Tammy's the whole time?"

She didn't remember hearing the phone. "I must have been asleep," she said. "I came home at lunch. I didn't . . . well, I didn't feel very well."

"Are you all right?"

"I ate too much, as usual, that's all. I'm fine now. I can handle it."

"Good. Listen, love, Mother's not feeling well, either, so I'm going to stick around until I know she's okay. Dad's helpless around here. He thinks it's a mortal sin when somebody catches a cold."

"You baby her, Michael," though it was said without rancor.

"I know, I know."

"You'll call me?"

"Every day. Hey, it's not like I'm in California or anything. I'm only in Hartford."

"It's still too far away."

"You're telling me. Happy, love?"

"I'd be happier if you were here."

"So would I. Damn, I think she's trying to get out of bed. Stubborn old coot. If she had pneumonia she'd try the Boston Marathon if we weren't looking. Take care, darling. I love you."

She said "I love you" to a phone that was dead.

But that's all right, she told herself as she warmed up the kettle for a last cup of tea. That's all right. He loves me. He'll help take care of me. Anything I can't handle Michael will, for sure.

She drank it slowly, until she told herself she was stalling. Then she washed her hands twice, brushed her hair at her reflection in the back-door pane, and dialed Paul's number, her right hand drumming on the wall. But the man who answered wasn't Paul Prescott.

"Windsor," he said when she demanded his name. "Ben Windsor. Who's this, please?"

"Dr. Melissa Redmond," she said. Windsor. Windsor. Damn, she knew that name as well as her own. Who the . . . police. Ben Windsor was a cop. "Officer, I'm sorry. I think I've dialed the wrong number."

"If you were trying to get the Prescotts, no you didn't."

She fumbled for the chair and pulled it to her, sat heavily. "What . . . I don't understand."

She listened until the policeman was finished, answered several questions in toneless monosyllables, rang off and traced a design on the wall.

It was that stupid glass screen set into the fireplace. The poice still weren't sure exactly how it happened, but sometime during the evening (sirens . . . sirens . . .) pressure had built up behind it, finally exploded it into the room. Paul and Tammy were lying on the hearth. Naked. Fire and glassknives sorched and punctured, blistered and slashed. Paul's jugular had been severed; Tammy was in the hospital, not expected to live.

(sirens . . . sirens . . . and carolers smiling)

"It's all right, Mel," she told herself then. "Don't panic. This is real, it isn't the darkman. What you have to do now is get ready. Wash. Dress. Walk to the hospital (one block up, three blocks over). Do everything you can for Tammy. Then call Michael to see what the legalities are. Legalities." She grinned at the word. Anyone who could remember a word like that at a time like this could handle anything. Anything at all. Including madness.

With a sharp nod she hurried up the stairs, undressed, showered, washed and dried her hair, stood in front of the mirror for several minutes trying to decide what makeup to use, went into her bedroom and threw off the bath towel, sat in the middle of the bed and crossed her legs.

Stared at the front window until it was dark.

Stared at the front window until the moon rose.

Stirred and called the hospital. Using her title she found out Tammy had fallen into a coma which she was not expected to leave. Mel sighed and hoped the end would be peaceful. An hour later she called again . . . the end had been quiet.

The telephone rang.

Be happy, Melissa.

And just before midnight she knew she was sane.

It surprised her, her sanity. There was no sudden fireball of revelation of thunderous voice from a fire-breathing cloud or chorus of angels from a pillar of fire. It . . . just . . . came. She had started walking around the house aimlessly, bumping into furniture, knocking against walls, when a particularly sharp corner dug into her calf. She yelled. She swore. She picked up a vase and threw it into the tree. When it rattled, trembled, began to fall, she lunged at it frantically, her hands plunging into the branches to grab the the trunk. Closed her eyes and waited. Righted the tree and knelt on the carpet to wipe the sap and the needles away from her fingers. As she did so, she bumped into some of the presents.

Frowned and picked one up and shook it. Then she tore open the wrapping and tossed the empty box aside. Twice more she did the same before rocking back to her heels and uttering a quicksharp laugh. Empty. What an idiot! A lot of empty presents and no one around to accept them, or deny them, or call her a fool for pretending she had things that never existed.

I'll be damned, she thought. I'll . . . be . . . damned.

Biology, of course, dealt with those things that grew and were living. Bio. The study of life. Her life. Plant life. Even the life she had given the darkman.

Study him, fool; and she knew she was sane.

Cause and effect, isn't that the way it is? She nodded to herself and sat full on the floor. Cause: unhappiness. Cause: Sam Litten and his amorous pursuit and his threats to her career. The effect was simple: Sam Litten had to go. She frowned. Had she really been happy when Sam died? No, she decided, not right away, but deep down inside something stirred, something was pleased that a pressure had been lifted, a pressure was gone. Cause, then: unhappiness. Cause: Tammy and Paul playing with her mind—the one accusing her of fomenting infidelity, the other accusing her of seeing things that weren't there. Effect: Tammy and Paul Prescott had to go. She frowned again. Paul had—right away, according to the police. But not Tammy. Think, she ordered as she held her head in her hands, pressing her palms to her temples. Think. Think. Cause: unhappiness. Cause: Tammy in a coma, never to see the snow or the sunlight or the moonlight again. Effect: Tammy . . . went.

Mel scrambled to her feet and looked out the window. There was no one in the street, no one standing in the snow that drifted out of the dark.

And as suddenly as she had known she was perfectly sane, she knew exactly why the darkman wasn't there: she was happy. She was content. Of course, there was sorrow for the loss of her friends, but that was something you lived with because sorrow didn't last.

"Happy," she whispered. And smiled. Then grinned.

When Michael returned she would command them to be married. He'll agree. They'll tie the knot. They'll live in this house and raise a hundred children. One of these days she might even head the department. Maybe even be dean.

Her laughter took the house, and the darkness, like a comet. Followed her up to her bed like its tail.

Under the covers, then, the quilt to her chin. The sheets cool, the pillow soft, the moon closing her eyes.

And after the honeymoon, she decided before sleeping, she would tell Michael of her partner, and what the darkman had done.

She prayed Mike would believe her.

She never looked good in black.

EPILOGUE

And it is still raining.

It seems as if it has always been raining.

I've put the book on the floor beside my chair and have moved to stand at the window, to look out across the street through panes that tremble like nervous ice at the passing of the wind. There are streaks of oil-induced rainbows writhing along the blacktop, and there are dark holes in the pavement that mark the spread of agitated puddles. The lamppost opposite me provides a glow that is more fog than light, and through it slashes leaves pursued by the wind, and rain more like scratches on an ancient, museum film. It is too late for automobiles, too late for pedestrians; my neighbor down the road has forgotten again to turn off the yellow bulb over his front porch, and the old man on the corner has left his empty garbage can out by the curb where it twirls like a drunken dwarf, kept from falling only by the battered lid that has somehow jammed at its base.

Twice in the last hour since reading the last line I've walked to the telephone to call Natalie, or Marc, but each time I've stopped because I have no idea what to say. Certainly, absolutely, I do not believe a single word in that volume, nor do I really understand why Nat wanted me to see what she'd gotten. She surely can't believe it either; she's too level-headed for that. And Marc has a successful newspaper to run; he can't be bothered with postmidnight calls from a fool who lives alone.

In fact, the more I think about it, the more I realize it would be just like them to have set all this up ahead of time, just waiting for the right sort of weather and for me to be in the right sort of mood. They probably went to bed hours ago, holding each other in silent rollicking laughter and wondering how long it would be before I confronted them, sheepishly, with what they had done to my peace of mind.

It would be just like them.

And it would be just like me to fall for it without question.

So why don't I stop staring at the rain and call them and be done with it. Why don't I just walk over there and pick up the receiver and call them and get myself to bed. Why don't I just do that little, inconsequential thing.

Because there's a problem. Rather, I'm still not sure exactly how much of a problem there is. If there is one. If I'm not just letting the rain and the wind and the leaves crawling over the porch get on my nerves, which is precisely what the Claytons would be after . . . if there were all an elaborate, and expensive, joke.

You see, there is a place called England's, for example. It is a brokerage firm, it's still down there on Centre Street, and is run now, I believe, by a distant cousin to the founder. Samantha (who is definitely no figment of anyone's imagination) eloped, I'm told, with a man named Bartelle, from Harvard, and the house she occupied while she was in the village is deserted now, falling apart, one of those places boys like to visit now and again to test their courage for girlfriends who look on in wide-eyed admiration (and with secret, knowing grins). This is all part of village lore. Every village has its scandals, and Oxrun is no different in that regard.

Like Jameson the postmaster, who murdered all those people and took off for parts unknown. It's been ten years, but every so often Abe Stockton will take out the file and have Marc run a short piece about it, thinking perhaps that someone, somewhere, will recognize the man and finally turn him in.

And then there's Melissa Wister (nee Redmond), who married a lawyer whose name may well have been Michael, and left him dead in their bed just a couple of years ago. The word is she took the last train from the depot that very night, destination (so the stationmaster said) . . . west. No foul play indicated. The man's heart simply stopped. Cold.

The Cock's Crow is still out there on Mainland Road, too. Grace Hancock has often treated me to a drink now and then, and lays in a supply of Guinness when I'm feeling expansive. I've never seen her husband. Nobody talks about him, not even the bartender.

None of that, of course, proves a damned thing except that whoever wrote the book certainly knew his or her history, and wasn't above twisting it a little here and there to create a sensation where none really exists.

It is, the whole project, in its elaborate way admirable.

So why don't I call Nat and get it the hell over with?

I don't know. I honest to god don't know.

I stand at the window, hands in the pockets of my robe after cleaning my glasses for the fifth or sixth time and lighting still another cigarette that, for some reason or other, I don't bother to finish. The rain is still falling (sheeting now against the window), the wind has found a crack under the front door (it's colder than before) and the house has filled with shadows that bring with them distant whisperings.

Later, then. I guess I'll call Nat later. After the rain has stopped, and the wind has stopped, and daybreak has put an end to the evening.

That'll be the best thing.

Meanwhile . . . I stand at the window, with the book shimmering behind me, and I see each time the wind shifts the indistinct figure of someone standing just outside the reach of the streetlight, of someone darker than shadow in the corner of my porch, of someone waiting on the lawn, oblivious to the storm.

I see it.

But I don't believe it.

> *Charles L. Grant*
> Oxrun Station
> 1981